WATCH
OVER
ME

WATCH OVER ME

NINA LACOUR

Dutton Books

DUTTON BOOKS

An imprint of Penguin Random House LLC, New York

First published in the United States of America by Dutton Books,
an imprint of Penguin Random House LLC, 2020

Visit us online at penguinrandomhouse.com.

Library of Congress Cataloging-in-Publication Data is available.

Printed in the United States of America

ISBN 9780593108970

1   3   5   7   9   10   8   6   4   2

Edited by Julie Strauss-Gabel

Design by Anna Booth

Text set in Carre Noir Std

For Kristyn

WATCH
OVER
ME

had we been telling the truth

ON THE MORNING OF MY INTERVIEW I slept until eight, went downstairs to the kitchen, and poured myself the last of the coffee. I stood at the counter, watching out the window as I sipped, and then pushed up my sleeves and turned on the water to wash the breakfast dishes that Amy and Jonathan had left stacked in the sink.

In just a few days, I would leave them.

Amy had bought a crib and tucked it into the garage. A few days after that, she came home with a bag from a toy store. A stuffed bunny peeked over the side. She asked me how my English final went and I told her that I wrote about the collapse of social mores in a couple of short stories and she said it sounded great. And then she took the bag into their bedroom as though it were nothing.

She was only being kind. I knew that. They hadn't asked me to stay.

The sink was empty. I scrubbed it until it was perfectly

white and then I turned off the water. I tried to breathe. I tried not to want this so badly.

My phone buzzed.

"Are you ready?" Karen asked. She'd been my social worker for four years and even though I could tell she was in traffic, probably dribbling coffee on her skirt and checking her email as she talked to me, she calmed my racing heart.

"I think so," I said.

"Remember—they read your letter. I've told them so much about you. They've talked to all your references. This is just a final step. And you get to make sure you really want it."

"I want it."

"I know you do, honey. I want it for you too. Call me as soon as it's over."

He knocked at ten thirty, exactly when he said he'd arrive.

"Mila?" he asked when I opened the door. He stuck out his hand. "Nick Bancroft. So nice to finally meet you."

I led him into the kitchen, where a round table sat beneath a window in the sun and the chairs were close enough for friendly conversation but far enough apart for strangers.

"How are you doing?" he asked after we sat.

"Well, finals are over, so that's good," I said.

"Yes, congratulations. Your transcripts are solid. Have you considered college?"

I shrugged. "Maybe I'll go at some point."

He nodded, but I saw that he felt sorry for me. My eyes darted to the window. I didn't know how to talk about my life with someone who understood. I clenched a fist in my lap and forced myself not to cry. I was ready to prove my work ethic, talk about the hours I spent volunteering at the library, and assure him that I was not afraid of dirt or messes or children throwing tantrums—but I was not ready for this.

"So, let me tell you about Terry and Julia and the farm," he said, taking mercy on me. "They adopted me when I was three, so it's been home basically all my life. I haven't lived at the farm in a long time, but I help them run the finances and I do all the interviews." I felt my fist unclench and I settled into the chair and listened to him tell me about the things I had already learned from talking to Karen and reading a *San Francisco Chronicle* article from fifteen years ago with the headline MENDOCINO COUPLE ADOPTS FORTIETH FOSTER CHILD. He talked about the farm and how everyone contributes to running it, from the children to the interns, and how as an intern I would spend my weekdays teaching in the school-house and my Sundays waking up at five a.m. to run the booth at the farmers' market. He told me about the holidays when all the grown-up children come back to visit. "It becomes home if you let it," he said. "Even for the interns. I know that might sound hard to believe, but it's true."

"When do I find out?"

"Oh!" he said. "I thought you knew. You've been chosen already. It's yours if you want it."

My hands flew to my face. "Thank you," I said. And then I couldn't say anything else. He nodded, that look of sympathy again, and kept talking.

"Most of your hours will be spent in the school. They've designed a curriculum and your job will be to learn it and teach the six- to nine-year-olds. There is only one of them right now, I think, but more will come soon. And Terry and Julia will be there to help."

"Would you like some tea?" I blurted. I had meant to ask him when he got there but had been too nervous. Now that I knew I was chosen, I wanted him to stay and tell me everything. Maybe that way I could hold it inside me—a real, live thing—in the days between that one and the one of my arrival.

"Sure," he said. I filled the kettle and set some boxes in front of him. He chose peppermint, and as I poured the steaming water over the leaves I breathed in the scent and it was like starting over already.

"I want to make sure you understand what this is," Nick said. "Quite a few people have turned it down. And some people haven't known what they were getting into and it hasn't worked out. You need to *want* it. It's a farm. It's in the middle of nowhere—to one side is the ocean and in every other direction is nothing but rocky hills and open land. It's almost always foggy and cold and there's no cell service and no town to shop in or meet people— Mendocino is forty-five minutes away. Farmers'-market days are the only times you'll interact with the outside world, and you'll be weighing squashes and wrapping flowers most of the time."

"That's fine," I said. "I don't mind."

He warned me that the cabins where the interns live were tiny, only one room with wood-burning stoves for heat. He said that there was a landline but no cell service, and that everyone ate meals together three times a day and took turns with prep and cleanup.

"The main house is comfortable and you're always welcome in it. They have tons of books and a bunch of instruments. There's even a grand piano in the living room."

"I've always wanted to play the piano," I said. I don't know why I didn't tell him about all my years of lessons and the songs I knew by heart. "Someone to Watch Over Me" began to play in my brain, and the kitchen filled with music. My grandmother was sitting next to me, her fingers showing me where my fingers should go. Nick kept talking, and I listened over the sound of piano notes, full and rising. I had been so young. I didn't tell him about the terrible thing I'd done. He didn't ask those kinds of questions. Funny, when interviewing for a job to work with children, that a person would ask about college and remoteness and not say, *Tell me* _the worst thing you ever did. Tell me about your wounds. Can I trust you?_

Had they known the truth about me they might not have given me the job, I thought, even though I was determined to be good. Even though I held on fiercely to my own goodness.

By the time he finished his tea, we had it all planned out. He asked if I wanted to wait until after the graduation ceremony and I said no, that I didn't care about wearing a hat and robe and walking with the other students. Okay, he said, then he would pick me up on Sunday and we would drive up together. He gave me a thin volume called _Teaching School: A Handbook to Education on The Farm_ and asked me to read it. He said, "Mila, I have a good feeling about this. I think you'll be a perfect fit with all of us." And I told him I had a good feeling about it, too. And I told him that I felt lucky, and he said, "You _are_ lucky. We all are."

And then he left.

———

Had we been telling the truth, he would have said, _The place where I'm sending you—it looks beautiful, but it's haunted._

Okay, I would have said.

It will bring everything back. All that you tried to bury.

I understand.

It's going make you want to do bad things.

I have experience with that.

And how did it turn out?

Terribly. But I promise to do better this time.

We could have had that conversation—it would not have been impossible. I would not have told him everything about me, but I would have told him enough. I still would have taken that four-hour drive up the jagged coastline to be with Terry and Julia and Billy and Liz and Lee and the rest of the children. All I'm saying is it would have been easier had I known.

FROM MY UPSTAIRS BEDROOM WINDOW, I watched for Nick's shiny black car. Once it appeared, I stood and set my cell phone on the windowsill. I didn't expect Amy and Jonathan to keep paying the bill, and there was no service where I was headed anyway. I took one final look at the room from the doorway—drawers empty now, bed stripped—and then I went downstairs.

I said goodbye to Amy and Jonathan and promised to send letters as we loaded the little I owned into the trunk.

"I hope the baby is sweet," I said to Amy. Her eyes darted away, but there was nothing for her to feel guilty over. They had let me live in their house for three of the four years I had been in the foster system. They'd given me a nice room and cooked me food and talked with me and bought me everything I needed. It was nobody's fault that we didn't fall in love. They were young and they wanted a baby.

"I mean it," I said.

I climbed into Nick's car and waved goodbye. The finality

of it all rose over me. I was *leaving*. My vision went dark, the world stopped. But then it passed, and I was all right.

Five hours later, Nick turned off Highway One and onto an unmarked gravel drive. He avoided potholes for a quarter mile, and slowed as we approached a wide wooden gate.

"For the goats," he said.

He stopped the car, opened the door to climb out, and left the engine running.

It was just before eight o'clock and the sky was pale pink, and I watched through the windshield glass as he unlatched the gate and pulled one side open, then crossed in front of the car to open the other. Behind him was a field and a big wooden barn. Some moss-covered boulders. Two goats munching grass.

Here I was.

I had made it.

And then he was back in the car, and we rolled forward. When he stopped again, I said, "I'll get it," and I stepped onto the farm for the first time. It was salty and muddy and cold—even in June—and I breathed in its newness as I swung the gates closed and latched them shut. When I turned back to the car, I could see a row of small cabins, and past them, a sprawling farmhouse with its lights on, all white and three stories, something from a picture book or an old movie, nothing like any house I'd ever set foot in.

"See that over there?" Nick asked, pointing to a curved, white tent. "That's the flower tunnel. Julia's famous around here for her flowers."

"I can't wait to see everything."

He parked midway down the gravel drive, at the closest point to the cabins, and we walked across the field, Nick with my suitcase, me with my backpack and duffel. The cabins were identical from the outside—each of them tiny, more sheds than houses—with small front windows and old brass doorknobs. Some muffled words followed by laughter came from inside the first cabin as we passed it. About twenty paces later we reached the second, which was silent and still. And then after another twenty steps, he stopped in front of the last one.

"Welcome home," Nick said.

He made no move to open the door, so I turned the knob myself. I expected the inside to be dark, but it wasn't. A skylight cut through the middle of the ceiling, casting the room in the same pink glow as outside.

Nick tucked my suitcase just inside the doorway. My shoes were muddy from the field, so I set my backpack and duffel inside without crossing the threshold. I saw a rug, a twin bed with a wrought-iron frame, a writing desk with a chair, a wood-burning stove, and a stack of cut wood.

"I've always liked these little cabins," he said. "But I never got to live in one. They're only for the interns."

"You lived in the house?"

He nodded. "In a room with two other boys. We whined about it all the time—we were total shitheads—but it was great. Now we meet up for vacations every summer and we always share a hotel room. I never sleep as well as I do when I'm in a room with my brothers."

I smiled. "That's sweet," I said.

"I'm going to head over to the house, but take your time. Terry or Julia will show you how everything works a little later."

"Okay. I'll see you soon."

I waited for a moment longer, there in the doorway.

Then I took off my shoes, lined them neatly by the threshold, stepped into the cabin, and closed myself in. The rug was soft underfoot and full of color—greens and pinks and blues. And even without a fire in the stove, I was warm.

I could have stayed there for the rest of the night, but they were waiting for me. After I'd sat on the bed to test its softness and hung my clothes on the tiny rack between the woodstove and the table, I slipped my shoes back on and headed across the field.

I approached the main entrance, but the windows on each side of the heavy oak door were dark. So I walked the perimeter of the house, running my hand along the white wood planks until I heard voices and saw light, and found a small patio with a door to a mudroom that opened onto a kitchen. It swung open before I finished knocking.

There was Julia, for the first time.

She had a soft body and laugh lines, white-blond hair and pink lips. "This is home," she said. "No knocking on doors here. Just come right in."

She wound her arm through mine and led me in. I had expected more people but apart from us it was only Nick and Terry, leaning toward each other from opposite sides of a butcher-block island, immersed in conversation.

"Ah," Terry said when he saw me. He had silver close-cropped hair and brown skin, a wide white smile, and eyes that surprised me with their blueness. "Mila, welcome. I'm sure you're hungry. We saved some dinner for you and Nick."

He put a mitt on his hand, opened an old-fashioned oven, and pulled out two plates heaped with mashed potatoes and sausages and beans. He lit the burner to warm some gravy in a small cast-iron pot.

"Special occasion food, I see," Nick said. Then, to me, "Prepare yourself for a *lot* of soup."

Terry laughed, reached an arm toward Nick, and ruffled his hair.

"I'm not *twelve*," Nick said, laughing, too.

Terry turned to me and smiled, warm but careful. "Here, sit."

I sat at the never-ending kitchen table, all oil-spotted

and cup-stained, and let the dinner fill me up while Terry and Julia chatted with Nick about his new job in a San Francisco skyscraper. I half listened, taking in the details of the kitchen. The blue-and-white-flowered curtains, the butcher-block counters, the giant mason jars lined up on shelves, full of flour and cornmeal and sugar and rice. I had never been anywhere like it.

"Well . . . ," Nick said when he had finished eating.

"You're sure we can't persuade you to stay?" Terry asked.

"Gotta work in the morning. But I'll come up again soon. Good luck," he said, giving me a quick hug goodbye. "Don't let these two work you too hard."

They walked him out, and by the time they returned I was also finished eating.

"Mila," Terry said, picking up my empty plate and water glass. "Why don't you stay and visit with us for a little bit before I show you around."

"I'd love to," I said. "Can I can help clean up?"

"Oh, don't worry about these. You'll be cleaning up plenty soon enough." He set my dishes in the sink and smiled as he nodded toward the living room, where I could see that Julia was already arranging pillows on one of the sofas. I followed him up the two steps that separated the rooms. A fire burned under a grand hearth, glowing across overstuffed chairs and floor pillows, two sofas and a grand piano. The whole room was covered in floor-to-ceiling shelves laden with books and framed photographs. Rugs piled upon rugs. Everything was beautiful and nothing was perfect, and I didn't know how I could have been chosen to be there.

Julia sat on the sofa, one leg tucked under. "Nick said you had an easy drive up. Have you been this far north before?"

I chose one of the chairs and sank into it. "No," I told her. "Never this far." I traced the outline of a bird printed on the armrest. I was trying not to look at the grand piano, which filled up the corner behind her. The sight of it made my chest ache.

The fire crackled and light danced across the ceiling and I wanted to give them something of myself. "I have to tell you . . ." They both leaned forward. "Nick told me about the piano. And for some reason I said I wanted to learn how to play it, but I actually *know* how to play. It's just been a very long time."

Julia laughed. "It's funny, isn't it? The things that come out of our mouths."

"I'm glad you told us," Terry said. "What a treat to have someone here who plays well. There's enough terrible playing, believe me."

"I don't know if I play *well*. It's been years."

"Do you want to play now?" Julia asked.

I did want to. I wanted to very badly. So I got up and

walked across the room and sat down and set my fingers on the keys.

I remembered what to do next. It came back to me. I played "Someone to Watch Over Me" from beginning to end without faltering. I knew just which keys to press, when to pause, and when to speed up. I played softly because, upstairs, children were sleeping. I finished and crossed back to the chair. I wondered if they could see me blushing, but I didn't really mind if they did.

"We knew we picked well," Julia said.

"Yes," Terry said. "Now tell us who taught you to play like that."

So I told them that I had lived with my mother and my grandparents for most of my childhood, until I turned thirteen and my mom and I moved in with Blake. "My grandmother loved to play the piano and she was a really good teacher. I don't even remember trying to play, or messing up, or worrying about whether I was doing it right. I just remember her fingers on the keys and her telling me to follow."

"And what happened to your grandparents?" Terry asked.

"They died sometime after we moved out. In a car accident."

"And we heard that your mother . . ." Julia trailed off, waiting for me to finish the sentence.

"She left," I said. "After the fire." I traced the bird again, and then the branch it perched on, and the leaves that sprouted from the branch. By the time I looked up I was able to meet their faces. "I don't want to talk about the fire if that's okay."

"That's just fine," Julia said.

"Your past is your own," Terry said.

I nodded. We sat quietly for a minute or two. Julia said, "Thank you for playing for us. Thank you for your openness." She stood up and stretched her arms over her head. "It's past nine already. I'm going to check on the children. They're so looking forward to meeting you in the morning."

"I'm looking forward to meeting them, too."

"Let's get you some provisions," Terry said. "It's always nice to have something in case you want a midnight snack without crossing the field. And then we'll go to your cabin and I'll show you how to heat it."

In the kitchen, he handed me a basket and offered me oranges and a loaf of bread and cookies. "And now," he said, once the basket was full, "we cross the field to the third cabin." He gestured to the window, then stopped. I followed his gaze but at first all I saw was our reflection, standing beneath a light in the kitchen: a tall Black man with an expression of wonder, a lonely white girl trying to make sense of the dark.

Then in the moonlight I saw something outside, glowing and crossing the field, moving closer. And the closer it came, the more it looked like a figure, like how a person would look if a person emanated light.

"I hope you aren't afraid of ghosts," Terry said.

I felt gripped around the throat at first. Felt a familiarity. A darkness. My spine went stiff and straight and I made my face blank. I would be impenetrable. I would not give myself away.

The ghost hovered in place on the moonlit field. It lifted its arms to the sky and spun in a slow circle. A girl, I thought, by the way she moved. And, in spite of myself, I was mesmerized.

"No," I whispered. "No, I'm not afraid."

I didn't know if I was telling the truth.

All I knew was I wanted to watch her spin forever. I wanted to *be* her. The soft, dark grass on my bare feet. Free of the fears I carried with me. We watched her, Terry and I did, until she had spun herself invisible. What a wonder it was, to stand side by side with someone and watch the same thing. And then all that was left was an open field and a moon and some cabins in the distance.

"Julia and I were warned before we bought this place that there were ghosts here. We didn't believe it, or maybe we didn't care. But the first time I saw them, I dropped to my knees."

I turned toward him, waited for more. But he shook his head as though to break the memory. "Shall we?" he asked.

The mudroom was stocked with raincoats and boots and a full shelf of battery-powered lanterns. He handed a lantern to me and took one for himself. "Whenever you head into the dark, bring one of these with you. The paths are uneven and the field can get muddy. Keep one in your cabin and then bring back the others when you return to the house."

We stepped out and crossed right through the space where the ghost had been. I thought there would be something—a scent, a breeze—but she was gone completely and the night was only the night.

"We'll start with the bathroom," he said, striding past the row of three cabins to a smaller structure behind them. "The door sticks sometimes. Push down a little bit. Lean into it."

I tried and it worked. It was a simple, clean space with a toilet and a counter with a sink and a new bar of soap.

"It gets very cold. Not quite ideal for the middle of the night, but I hung this hook on the back of the door in case you wear a jacket over. The shower is around back." We held out our lanterns and walked the perimeter of the building to a high gate that enclosed a patio of sorts. First there was a bench and several hooks. A few steps over was a shower-head, and next to that was a round, metal trough, the kind that animals might drink water from. I realized it functioned as a bathtub. "It is not the most comfortable, but it does the trick if you want a soak," Terry said. "And you're welcome to bathe in the house anytime."

Back at my cabin, he stood at the doorway. "I'd like to show you a couple of things. How to light the fire, where to stack the wood. Do you mind if I come in?"

"Not at all."

He checked the supply of wood. "Oh, good," he said. "Billy made sure you had plenty. You'll meet him and Liz tomorrow, along with all the children. Breakfast is at seven thirty in the kitchen. Have you used a wood-burning stove before?" he asked.

"No," I said.

"The best way to learn is by doing," he told me. "So go ahead and take two logs from the pile and a few sheets of that newsprint."

I did as I was told, placed them in the stove. He took a matchbook from a blue dish, began to hand it to me, and then froze—his arm in mid-reach, the matchbook between his fingers. I didn't look at his face but I could see him breathing. My heart lunged into my throat—*he is afraid of me, afraid of me*—but then I remembered that he didn't know the whole story, so he had no reason to be afraid. He was sorry for me, then. He thought it might be difficult.

"I don't mind," I told him. "I'm not afraid of fire."

"Good, good," he said. I took the matchbook from his fingers, tore off a match, and struck it. After the newsprint was lit, I closed the doors of the stove and latched them.

"Just one more thing and then I'll go."

I waited.

"You're free to leave anytime. You are not a prisoner here. But if you *do* want to leave, all I ask is that you let us know so that we can drive you into town. Some people have set out walking. It isn't safe."

I nodded.

"Of course, I hope you'll stay," he said, and smiled.

"I plan to," I told him, and we said good night.

I unzipped my duffel, pulled out my toiletry bag, and walked the path to the bathroom to prepare for bed. When I was heading back, the ghost had reappeared on the green. She leapt, she spun. I averted my eyes. Heard Terry saying, *I hope you aren't afraid of ghosts.* My pace quickened as I approached my cabin. I shut the door fast and hard behind me.

I undressed and stepped into my pajamas, pulled the covers back and climbed in. My face touched the pillow.

Musty sleeping bag on a concrete foundation. My mother tucking me in.

Framed rooms, but no roof. Stars overhead. Dying eucalyptus trees, towering above.

A hint of smoke wafted from the firepit below as my mother leaned over me. She pressed her soft lips against my forehead.

"It's like camping," she whispered, zipping the bag to my chin. "Sweet dreams."

She stood. She turned. She left me alone in that strange, cold place.

But no, no—I was in my cabin. Its walls and roof. Desk and duvet. Fire burning to keep me warm.

I covered my pounding heart with my hand.

"This is my home," I said to myself.

I found my way back—to the soft pillow under my cheek, to the glow of the moon through the skylight, to the steadiness of my breath.

"This is my home," I whispered as I shut my eyes. "All the rest is over."

the schoolhouse

IN THE MORNING I OPENED THE CURTAINS to fog so thick and low on the grass that I couldn't see the house beyond it. With the fire out, my cabin was cold, no trace left of last night's warmth.

I put on my sweater to head to the bathroom. I hadn't considered the possibility of running into anyone, but here were the other interns, headed right toward me.

Liz and Billy. Her, with short dreads and dark skin and a nose ring, smiling at me. Him, lanky and fair in a jean jacket and carefully slicked hair, as though he had sprung to life from a James Dean poster.

"You must be Mila," Liz said as they drew near. She wore only a towel beneath her jacket.

"Yes," I said, thinking of my tangled hair and sour breath. I thought they would stay to talk but they blew past me. Billy turned and walked backward a few steps. "See you at breakfast," he said, and we went on in our separate directions. *Had they showered together?* I wondered. *Or had they met on the path, coincidentally, as we just had?* I would check the mirror in my room before leaving next time. I wished for my own bathroom. Scolded myself for my ingratitude.

There I was, on the beautiful rocky coastline, with a cabin of my own and a job and hot meals every day. There I was, with the prospect of a family. And I was worried about my hair and my breath. We are all humans; we all wake up messy and confused. It was nothing, I told myself. Get ready. Go on with your day.

I felt so self-conscious, appearing in the doorway for break-fast, all those faces turning to take me in. *Jackson, Emma, and Hunter. Darius, Blanca, Mackenzie, and James.*

I would have to hear each of their names again and again to learn them. The three high schoolers sat in the far corner. Emma flashed me a bright smile. Hunter smirked and Jackson barely glanced at me at all. We were so close in age. I was grateful that I wasn't assigned to teach them. Liz, though—now dressed in jeans and a T-shirt, eating an avocado half with a spoon—said, "Let's make Mila feel welcome, everyone," and, miraculously, Hunter nodded. Jackson lifted a hand to wave.

Darius, Blanca, Mackenzie, and James—the little ones—perched together in a row on a tall bench at one side of the table. They paid special attention to the cloth napkins on their laps. At each of their places, Terry was setting down small bowls of plain yogurt and a boy followed behind him with a larger bowl, spooning berries into the white.

"Lee's famous fruit salad," Terry said.

So this was Lee. He turned, and when he saw me, he set down the bowl.

"Hey!" Blanca shouted. "I want my berries!"

Lee's eyes widened, but Billy said, "It's okay, buddy. I got this. You go meet your teacher." In a low voice, Billy spoke to Blanca, and then I heard her say, "May I have my berries *please*?" and Billy say, "Certainly."

Lee stepped toward me and held out his hand. He was nine years old and small for his age. His hand was thin, but his shake was firm, as though he had been practicing. "My name is Lee," he told me. "I'm your only student for now."

Terry placed his broad hand on Lee's skinny shoulder.

"Lee's been eager to meet you."

"I'm not very good at math," Lee said. "But I like to read."

I sat on a chair so that I would not have to look down at him as we spoke.

"*What* do you like to read?"

"Everything."

"I have a feeling we're going to get along," I told him. I smiled, and his serious face turned into a grin, and it was so

sudden and surprising—that smile—that I felt tears spring
to my eyes. I blinked them away fast and turned to the table
where Julia had set an empty mug and was offering me
coffee.

The schoolhouse was the old barn I'd seen on the drive in,
one expansive room with a few salvaged wood tables and
chairs arranged throughout. One corner was set up for the
preschoolers with mats and pillows and toys to play with.
All the dolls were handmade, stitched eyes and mouths, tiny
dresses and pants dyed turmeric yellow and beet red. A little
city of wood-carved houses sat on a low shelf with matching
cars lined up as if at a stoplight.

With windows lining both long walls, the room was
filled with morning light. It was relaxed and spacious, a perfect place for learning.

I told Terry as much, and he said, "I'm glad. But you may
wish to suspend your praise for another moment . . . Now
we let you in on the secret of the supply closet."

He opened the closet doors to reveal shelves crammed
full of typical school stuff—ruled paper and graph paper,
protractors and calculators. And unexpected things, too.
Sheets of beeswax. More wood toys. A papier-mâché mobile
of the solar system with its strings tangled, bins with costumes spilling over their sides.

"One day I will sort through all of this. I told myself I'd

do it before you arrived. I told myself I'd do it before Billy and Liz arrived. So much for my good intentions! But anything you need should be in here. If it isn't, let Julia or me know and we will get it for you or find a good substitute."

"I'm sure this will be more than enough," I said.

"We try to always have at least two kids of around the same age so they have someone to do lessons with. For a time, we had Esther along with Lee, but then Esther's aunt came forward to adopt her. It doesn't usually happen that way for us—our children usually stay. But there are two girls who may be joining us soon. Eight-year-old twins whose mother's parental rights were just terminated. We're waiting to see."

I nodded.

"All right, enough with the orientation. You read the handbook, yes?"

"Cover to cover," I said.

"Wonderful. You can help Lee with his equations now. He's been doing a lot of self-guided work lately and he'll appreciate having someone dedicated to helping him."

Lee sat at a table at the far end of the schoolroom with his shoulders hunched.

"May I?" I asked, placing my hand on the empty chair next to him, and he nodded, moving his notebook closer to make more space for me. The notebook was covered with carefully formed numbers and equations and black boxes that confused me until I realized that instead of crossing or scribbling out his mistakes, he had blackened them so no hints of their specific wrongness remained.

"Long division," I said. "How is it for you?"

His brow furrowed. "Fine," he said. "Hard, I guess. I'm stuck on this one. I keep thinking I'm getting it right, but when I check in the book, it's wrong."

"Can I help you?"

"Sure," he said.

When he slid his notebook toward me, I saw his hands— olive skin with graceful fingers, each of them straight except for the ring finger of his right hand. That finger turned out above the knuckle where it had clearly been broken and left to heal on its own. I became aware, then, of the way I moved through the world. No unusual scars or crooked bones. Nothing about the way I looked at first glance that gave me away. I wondered who had done that to him. Who had left it untreated.

He must have noticed me looking because he moved his hands under the table. And it struck me how bad it felt to him, to have me look for too long. My face burned. I wanted so much to be good at this.

I gathered my hair as I would if I were putting it into a ponytail.

"Look," I said, showing him one of my earlobes and then the other. He leaned in, looked closely. I felt the intensity of his gaze, and felt, too, the weight of what I was showing him.

"Do you see how the holes aren't centered? Do you see how this one . . . is higher than this one?"

Lee nodded.

"I didn't get my ears pierced because I thought it would look pretty. I didn't get it done at a mall or in a shop. The person who did it, he did it to hurt me."

I had never spoken the words before, hadn't told anybody. Now Lee would know it forever, and it would bond us together, and I hoped he would never again feel like a spectacle of pain around me.

We held each other's gaze for so long that I knew it must have meant something. Finally, he nodded, brought his hands back to the table. I looked at the ruled paper, his painstaking numbers, the little blacked-in squares of wrongness.

"Okay," I said. "Let me see. It's been a long time since I've done this."

I asked him to walk me through the problem, at first because I needed to remember the steps of long division but then because I realized it was a good method, to have him explain it to me. I caught his mistake a step before he got there, and then when he reached that point in the problem, he hesitated and I smiled.

"Oh," he said. "It should be seven."

"Yes. Now keep going. Let's see what you get."

"Seventeen-point-five," he said. "I'm pretty sure . . ." He turned to the back of the book and showed me.

"You got it!"

"Yay!"

"Should we start the next one?"

He found the problem and wrote it in his notebook, taking time to make every number perfect. If it was a one, instead of drawing a straight line he included the angle at the top and the line at the bottom. Sevens, he crossed. He added tiny tails to the ends of his twos.

At the far end of the schoolhouse, a child began to cry. I turned and there was Billy crouched between two of the little ones, reminding them to take turns with the blocks. I glanced at Liz, who was leading a workshop with her high school students; each of them was reading an essay, scrawling comments in their margins. I felt the twoness of Lee and me. The only pair. I was all he had, so I'd need to do my best. I looked at the notebook again to see his progress but found none had been made. He was turned to the window, fear plain on his face.

I followed his gaze but all I saw was a foggy sky with a bright spot where the sun broke through. A tangle of colorful flowers. Two red birds darting and falling and rising again.

But when I turned back I saw that his eyes were unfocused. His face had lost its color; he was gritting his teeth.

"Lee," I said. "What is it?"

He didn't answer me. I couldn't tell if he'd even heard what I'd said.

"Lee," I said louder. I looked behind me, but all the others were focused on themselves. It was just Lee and me, and I had to get him through whatever this was. Gently, I placed my hand on his shoulder and he startled, turned to me.

"What did you see out there?" I asked him, making sure my voice was soft, making sure I seemed purely good and calm and concerned, that I was the kind of person he would want to be there with him as he went through whatever it was he was enduring.

"Was it a ghost?" I asked.

"No," he said. "The ghosts only come out when it's dark."

Julia entered the schoolhouse at three o'clock to ring a brass bell.

"Lessons are finished for the day," she said when the chime faded, and across the schoolroom chairs were pushed out, books were shut and stacked, paper and pencils were put away. The little ones lined up. Lee was up and out of his chair, placing his supplies in the cabinet. Everyone but me knew what to do.

"Mila, come walk with me," Julia said, and I was relieved to be called away. She led me down the gravel road toward the highway. The two goats chewed grass.

"They're stubborn little creatures," Julia said. "And strong, too. The white one's Annabelle; she'll tolerate petting. Percy is the brown fellow and he's got a mean streak. Now I've warned you."

"They're very cute."

"They are," she said. "And they serve their purpose well."

"Which is?"

"Eating the dry grasses. Keeping away the brush." She opened the gate. "We keep this closed so that they don't run off."

"Nick told me."

"Good old Nick. Of course he did. I thought I'd take you to the ocean so you know the best route."

"I didn't realize we could walk."

"We're very close. The trail isn't marked, though, so you need to know where you're headed."

We followed the rest of the path out to the highway, and Julia pointed out the trees and shrubs and taught me their names. "The little ones can remind you if you forget. Quiz them. It's part of the curriculum we developed for the preschool. People need to know where they fit in in the world. The first part of that relies on understanding what's around them. So we give them the language and let them explore. The intern we had before Billy didn't care much for nature, so we were glad when we found Billy last year. He spent a lot of time camping before his parents died. They were real adventurers—rock-climbing expeditions, backpacking trips—they taught him so much about nature that we barely had to fill him in on anything."

We reached the highway. "Cars come by very fast," she said. "So, when you're walking with the children be sure to take their hands and go quickly. One moment there can be no sign of a car and then, before you know it, one is coming right at you." We crossed and walked for no more than a couple minutes before the path ended and the rocks dropped straight off.

We were standing at the edge of a bluff, looking down at the ocean. I felt my knees go weak and it surprised me. I hadn't known there were new fears to discover.

She must have noticed how I felt, because she linked her arm through mine. Her thick wool sleeve made my cheap cotton sweater seem inadequate. I told her so, and she said, "We have lots of extra clothes in the house. Try the upstairs closets when you need anything. We have shoes in all sizes and jackets and sweaters and scarves and hats and other accessories. Also board games, supplies for bird-watching and foraging. Even some old posters and framed artwork if you want to decorate your cabin. Really, anything you can think of. Now, let's head down."

We walked along the bluff until it met a trail that was partially obscured by an ancient madrone tree, and there we began the descent. It was steep and rocky, but before long we were on the sand. Seagulls flew overhead. In the distance, a few people surfed.

"Do you swim?"

"Yes," I said. "I mean, I know *how* to swim if that's what you're asking."

"Do you do it well?"

"Not really. Just in pools, mostly. When I was a kid. My friend Hayley's family had one."

"This is what you need to know about the Pacific. One, it's freezing so you'll need a wet suit. We have them along with everything else in the upstairs closets. If you're going to do it, come with Terry or me. Or with Billy and Liz—they're both strong swimmers. There's a serious current here, so don't ever swim when the tide's coming in or going out. If you *do* happen to get caught in a riptide, though, what you'll do is this: Relax into it. Let it take you out. As long as you don't struggle, it will send you right back to shore. Understand?"

I nodded. We watched the surfers, watched the waves. The sky was clear and blue now, no traces of the morning's fog.

"Do you like it?" Julia asked. But I didn't know what she meant. All I saw was the deep blue-green water, the white foam against dark rock. The wildflower-studded cliffs, and the tall grasses in the wind. "Because it's magnificent," she said. "But I don't like it. It scares me."

"I guess I didn't know I was *allowed* to not like it." I felt foolish saying that, but it was true.

"I love the sound," Julia said. "The sight from a safe distance. A *far* distance. I like a view of the ocean, but not the actual thing of it. But Terry and many of the others—Billy and Liz, too—they love being up close. I think it helps drown out certain things for them."

I nodded. I didn't know what to say. I looked at all of it and asked myself how I felt, and I didn't have an answer.

JULIA AND I ENTERED THE HOUSE through the front door, the one I'd turned away from the night before. It opened into a foyer that led to the living room, where the high schoolers were helping the little ones, gathered around the coffee table with scissors and glue and sheets of colorful paper.

"Time to clean up!" said Emma, the girl who'd smiled at me that morning. I watched as each of the tiny children stacked the paper and put the caps back on the glue. Emma patted little Blanca on the head before she led the other two teenagers upstairs.

"Thank you!" Julia called after them. Then she turned to the children and marveled over their collages and cleanup. She promised them extra bubbles for their baths and they happily followed her out. "The others should be in the kitchen," she called back. I could hear voices from around the corner—Terry and Lee and Billy—deep in conversation. I took the steps down through the doorway.

Four loaves of sourdough sat cooling on the counter. Billy was shaking a jar of cream, turning it to butter.

"Oh, there you are," he said when he saw me. "Julia stole you away."

Lee glanced up from his comic. "Where did she take you?"

"To the ocean."

The sloshing sound ended. "Finally!" Billy said. He unscrewed the lid, set down the jar, and rubbed his bicep. I noticed a gold bracelet on his wrist, a simple chain. Terry uncovered a giant pot and the scent of tomato soup filled the kitchen. Lee licked his lips and said, "Yum-yum!"

Terry ladled the soup into bowls on the counter and placed the lid back on the pot. "Billy, how is that butter coming along?"

"Stirring in the salt," Billy said. "Patience, old man."

A little later, Liz appeared from the living room. She crossed to the sink and washed her hands before grabbing a bread knife. "How was your first day?" she asked without turning around.

"I enjoyed it," I said.

"You don't have to say that just because we're all here," Billy said.

"Agreed," said Terry. "First days are often difficult."

But I thought of it—the early morning and the breakfast and the pencil sharpening and the lessons, even the mistake of looking too long at Lee's broken finger, even his moment of fear—and I was sure I was telling the truth.

"I really did," I said.

Lee shut his comic. "Let's play high-low."

Liz finished slicing and I noticed that each piece of bread was perfect, as though she'd sliced hundreds of loaves. She set down the knife and said, "Sure, Lee. Let's. Want to go first?"

"My high was meeting Mila. It's been hard to not have a teacher for two whole months."

Warmth rushed to my chest. Here was this little boy, who wanted me.

"*My* high was meeting Mila," Liz said. She glanced at me and smiled. I felt myself blush. "Terry?"

"Hmmmm . . ." He brushed his hands on the front of his apron. "Well, I met Mila yesterday so I have to break this lovely pattern. But my high was watching Mila teach school. She's a natural. With teaching, you have it or you don't. You can still get by by learning the nuts and bolts of it, but that teacher instinct—it can't be taught."

It was almost too much to take, all this praise.

"Are you going to keep going?" Billy asked. "I thought we were playing high-low but this sounds like a lecture."

Terry threw up his hands. "Go ahead."

Billy set a bowl of fresh butter next to the bread. "Well, obviously my high was meeting Mila. Welcome to the farm. We're super happy to have you."

"Thank you," I said. "My high is right now."

"It's almost time to call the rest in," Terry said. "Lightning-bolt lows! Mine's the supply closet in the schoolhouse. Utter chaos."

"A blister on my toe," Liz said.

"Missed my parents like hell this morning," Billy said.

Lee leaned forward. "That thing happened to me again. I got scared in my throat and stomach."

I wondered why he would say it now, so clearly, when he hadn't said it then. I wanted to be someone he trusted.

"That was mine, too," I said. "Seeing you feel that way."

He gave me a smile. When I was his age, I had my grandparents. I had my mother. It wasn't until later that all of it changed. *Lee,* I thought, as the freshly bathed children filed in, as Emma and Hunter and Jackson took the far end of the table, as he chewed small bites of bread, swallowed his careful spoonfuls of soup. *I'll do whatever I need to earn your trust.*

And once the four loaves were eaten along with all the butter, once everyone's bowls were empty, and the pre-schoolers had practiced the songs they'd been learning, and we'd moved into the living room for a round of charades, Julia stood and said, "It's warm tonight. Anyone up for a moon romp?"

"Yes!" the children all yelled, and out they went with their lanterns into the night while the high schoolers settled on the back porch, two of them with guitars, and Billy and Liz and I cleaned up in the kitchen.

"Lee's gone through a lot," Billy said to me, later. "He gets panic attacks. He knows how to work through them. Just give him some time and he'll be okay."

We were walking back to our cabins, the three of us, each of us holding a lantern.

"Do you know what happened to Lee's parents?" I asked.

Liz said, "His dad's in jail. Probably forever. His mom OD'd a little over a year ago and died. He doesn't like talking about it, but he ended up telling Samantha the whole story."

"Samantha?"

"The intern who was here before you."

"Oh," I said. "Right."

Billy shook his head. "Poor Lee." I nodded and thought of his broken finger, his moment of fear. "Night, Mila," Billy said.

"Good night," I said.

And then he opened his door and Liz followed him in. I remembered the laughter from the night before. I wondered if they were together or if they were only friends. It didn't matter. Either way I was not one of them, despite the kind things they had said.

I continued a few paces toward my cabin but soon

stopped again. A glow appeared in the distance, beyond the house. *The dancing ghost*, I thought. But as it came closer I saw it wasn't one ghost, but several.

They assembled in the center of the field. They clasped hands, formed a circle. One of them darted into its center and then back out again. They broke into a line.

They were playing a game. Clasping and unclasping hands, following rules I couldn't make sense of. They were wondrous and I was unafraid. Under the steady moon, the fog moving across the sky like a living thing, I watched for a long time, astonished by how lucky I was to have been chosen. How incredible it was to be there in that strange, incomprehensible place. I saw the glow of a new ghost approaching, and something shadowy, too. Something there and then gone.

I half slept in Blake's skeleton house under the eucalyptus trees.

Wind through the dry leaves.

An owl's hoot, a cat's yowl. A scampering. My mother's moan.

Once it was light I rose to my feet, bladder full, and found the hole in the ground Blake used as a toilet. He'd told us about the ashes he poured over to get rid of the smell, but I smelled it anyway—pungent enough to turn my stomach. I squatted, held my breath. When I had finished, I rinsed my hands at the spigot. I washed my face and my hair, too, used a bar of soap because it's all I could find. I wrung my hair out, water dripping onto the dirt, and went to find my mother.

There she was, sharing a bench with Blake by the firepit.

He looked at me with his green eyes, his smile that had never been friendly, not even the first time I'd met him. His arm was around my mother, holding her in place.

"Good morning," he said.

My best friend, Hayley, the only friend I spent time with outside of school, was away at camp with no cell service.

I left her a message later that day, telling her to call me as soon as she could. But that evening, before she'd called me back, Blake took my phone away.

"We don't need these," he said. "What we need is human connection."

He was standing in fur-lined slippers on the concrete foundation, the frame of the house towering over him, the last of the evening light filtering through the place where the roof should have been.

My mother had just left for work. She would be gone all night.

"I want to show you something," he said, slipping my phone into his pocket. "Follow me."

I followed him to the space he called his room. There, tarps hung as walls with blankets lining them for insulation. Layered carpets spread over the concrete, and on top of some of them was his mattress. He opened a box and dug through it for a velvet pouch. Inside was a pair of mother-of-pearl opera glasses.

He handed them to me. "These can be a lot of fun," he said. "The old-fashioned kind. Let's fix some dinner and you can see what you find when you take the time to really look. You don't need screens. You need real life."

While he grilled vegetables on a barbeque outside the house, I gazed through the glasses at the sky. I saw the stars and the moon. Some birds flew by and I lost sight of them, then scanned down and there they were, on a telephone wire.

And below them was a window, lit up, with a family in the living room working a puzzle. I watched the father slip a puzzle piece over to a kid who was a little younger than me. I could have watched them for a long time, but it felt like spying. I knew I wouldn't want some strange girl peering in on me when I didn't know about it, even if she was only curious and didn't mean any harm.

I turned the glasses downward and that's when I saw her. A woman, ancient, with vacant eyes. She stood in a nightgown on the street. In one hand, she held a bouquet of oversize, plastic daisies. In the other, she held what looked like the gnarled roots of a tree. She was on the sidewalk, alone in the dark, staring at nothing.

"Blake," I said.

He was carving into wood with a pocketknife while he waited for the food to cook. "Mm-hm," he answered, eyes fixed on his project.

"Look at that lady," I said. He kept carving for a moment and then saw I was handing the opera glasses to him. He took them and I pointed down at the street. "What's she doing? Do you think we should help her?"

He lifted the glasses to his eyes and shifted the focus. He remained turned toward where I had been looking for a long time. I could see her even without the glasses, standing perfectly still, then swaying back and forth before growing still again.

"What lady?" Blake asked.

But he had been looking right there. He was still looking. And there she was.

"The old woman."

"I don't see an old woman."

"Right *there*," I said. "With the fake flowers and that other thing."

"I don't know what you're talking about," he said. "You must be tired, you should go to bed." He folded the opera glasses and dropped them back in their velvet pouch.

"But I haven't had dinner yet. It's still early." I couldn't tell how early it was, though. I didn't have my phone. I didn't own a watch.

"You're so tired you're seeing things," Blake said. "You don't feel right. Go lie down."

I did as he told me.

"You know . . . ," he said the next morning. We were warming water over the fire for coffee. "I had a thought about this so-called woman you saw last night."

"She was right there," I said. "It's so weird you didn't see her."

"I'm wondering—was she by any chance wearing a nightgown?"

"Yes!"

"And was her hair very short?"

"Yes, that was her."

"And were the fake flowers daisies, by any chance?"

"Yeah. Yeah I think they were."

He poured coffee beans into a hand grinder and turned the handle.

"Her name was Lorna," he said. "She lived in the house across the street for years. But she died last May."

The next time I saw her it was daytime and my mother was there. I had been reading but had grown hungry. I closed my book and stood and there she was, empty-handed this time, in the nightgown still.

My mother and Blake were sitting at the table together, looking over his architectural plans.

"Look," I said to them. They both stood and craned their necks.

"Poor—" my mother started.

"Mila. Poor Mila," Blake said. "Apparently she's being haunted. All I see is a street corner. Isn't that all you see, Miriam?"

My mother looked at Blake and then back to where my ghost was standing.

"Only a street corner," my mother said.

Blake pulled something out of his pocket. A small

box. "I found something for you," he told her. She opened the lid.

"Oh, they're beautiful! Mila, come see."

A pair of silver earrings. They looked heavy and old.

"I had to talk the lady at the shop into selling them to me." He took one from the box. "Let's see how they look on you."

My mother blushed. "It's been so long since I've worn any. I'm afraid the piercings might have closed up."

"We'll give it a try," Blake said, pressing the post to her earlobe. "Almost," he said. "Just needs a push."

I watched my mother wince and then smile, tears shining in her eyes.

"Next one," he said, and did it again. He wiped her blood from his hand. "Look at that, Miriam," he said. "You're a vision."

And then he turned to me. "Poor Mila," he said. "She feels left out." He scanned the surroundings before reaching to the ground. He closed his fist around a cluster of California poppies and pulled them from the earth. He handed them to me, dirty roots and all.

"Your consolation prize," he said.

I was in the dark again, on the farm again. Once my heart had steadied and I had caught my breath, I turned toward my cabin. For years, I'd done all I could to live a normal life, to forget the things that had happened, to leave the memories buried where they belonged—out of consciousness, obscured by neglect, unable to hurt me.

Why this now?

Here was the crunch of my shoes on the gravel, I reminded myself. Here was the lantern's light. One step and then another and soon I would be safe.

But as I turned the lock to my cabin door, I saw something below me, lying on the straw doormat.

California poppies, bound together with a blade of grass.

press it close

I ENJOYED THE DAYS THAT FOLLOWED — the feeling of working hard, learning to harvest, the soreness in my legs from all the crouching and kneeling. The farm's blackberry thickets and ocean views, whirring sprinklers, clusters of yarrow, and sweet peas climbing free over the fences. Soft grass under my feet.

Midweek, in the strawberry rows, a small gray cat took a liking to me, rubbed her strong little head against my legs.

"Meet Tulip," Julia said. "Every farm needs its cats to keep away the gophers."

On Thursday, Terry showed me how to nestle the summer squash into crates and the strawberry flats into boxes. Before night fell he sent me into the flower tunnel, Julia's domain. Rows and rows of flowers, in every color—muted and vibrant, subtle and showy—reached up from the earth. My breath caught at the beauty of it all. I had never seen flowers like these. Tiny green petals with bloodred centers. Blossoms of bright yellow and gold. Under the white, tentlike walls, Julia's hair glowed even whiter than usual. She held pruning shears in her gloved hands.

"I'm sorry, my loves," she said, and then she snipped the stems of the most beautiful flowers I had ever seen. All of them the colors of bruises. *Anemones*, she'd later tell me.

Night after night, when darkness fell, my heart quickened. But no new memories surfaced, nothing awaited me outside my door. The ghosts kept their distance and my relief was tinged with disappointment, as strange as that was to me. And again, I lay still under the skylight, awake and trembling. *They were only memories,* I told myself. I slept fitfully and was glad when morning came.

I crossed the field, nervous and eager, on the early evening of my first dinner shift. The sooner I learned how everything worked, the sooner I could feel truly a part of the rest of them. During the school day, when Lee had been doing some writing, I'd caught myself staring into the middle distance, imagining myself striding into the kitchen as though I belonged in it, cutting bread the way Liz did.

But now, I let myself in quietly through the mudroom door and peeked around the corner to see if anyone was there. Liz looked up from the kitchen table and waved, and I felt foolish to have hesitated. I wasn't even inside, and already my confidence was shaken.

Still, I knew how to cook. Maybe not the way they did, but enough to get by. I would not be so nervous over nothing, I resolved. And I stepped in.

"Come see what we're making," Liz said, so I joined her at the table.

She told me how Terry left instructions on the table for us, marked cookbook pages for the recipes he'd chosen. "Sometimes he leaves us cards with recipes," she said, showing me an index card, stained and water-buckled from use. "This one's for tonight."

I took it from her. Carrot soup.

"We make a *lot* of soup," she said. "Soup is easy. And see the basket on the counter over there?" On the counter by the sink was a tin bucket of carrots and celery, and next to it a basket full of heads of lettuce, radishes, and onions. "That's for the salad. Fresh from the garden."

"Amazing."

She shrugged. "You get used to it. So, it's simple tonight. It usually is when Terry leaves us in charge. When he feels like cooking one of his feasts, he joins us and bosses us around. But then he lets us take all the credit. You ready?"

"Yes."

Side by side at the counter, we worked. I peeled the just-harvested carrots for soup while Liz sliced radishes and onions for salad. We didn't talk at first, and I wondered if she was disinterested in me, if being assigned to cook with me instead of Billy was a disappointment. I cleared my throat. "So, you've been here a year?" I asked her.

She nodded.

"Has everyone been here so long?"

"Lee came a couple months after Billy and me. But otherwise, yeah."

"It seems nice here. I mean, everyone seems . . . nice."

"Yeah," she said. "They are."

I waited, hopeful, but she didn't say anything more. I added a carrot to my stack and picked up another. In the quiet between us, I drifted to the poppies on my doorstep the night before. Of the blossoms, how soft and light they had been in my palm when I'd lifted them from my mat. How harmless, how confounding. I'd looked out the window after locking my door, certain Blake would be there, staring back at me. I understood: I had come to live in a haunted place.

And then I flinched. Blood pooled on my finger. I had pushed the peeler too far and cut myself. I didn't cry out, didn't say anything, just crossed to the sink to run it under cold water. I thought Liz might not notice, but she disappeared to the bathroom and reappeared next to me with a cotton ball and a bandage. She took my hand and dried it.

"As you feel the pain begin, press it close and count to ten," she recited, pressing the cotton ball to the cut. "One . . .

two . . . three . . . four . . . five . . . six . . . seven . . . eight . . . nine . . . ten." I glanced at her face but felt heat rush to my own. We were so close. I turned my gaze to our hands. We both had short, smoothly filed fingernails. She wore a gold chain around her wrist. My own wrist was bare.

She removed the pressure. The cotton was red but the cut wasn't bleeding anymore.

"I've never heard that before," I said.

She wrapped the bandage around my finger. "Becky Anderson," she said. "Foster mother number three. For a little while I thought she might keep me."

Then she turned her back to me and finished her slicing. And I wanted to ask her to tell me more, wanted to confess that I had once shared those hopes. *Had we all?* I didn't know. But something in her posture, in the way she was suddenly humming a song as though to tune me out, told me that the moment had ended. So, it was back to dinner prep for us, not speaking unless it was to check the recipe.

But once everyone was seated on the benches around the massive kitchen table, spooning their soup and thanking us, Liz caught my eye from across the table and gave me a smile that was nothing if not genuine. It was warm, even. And I thought maybe I should have asked her more after all.

It was Sunday, market day. In the predawn darkness I'd awakened to the sound of Billy and Liz shuffling past my cabin. I'd heard them again a little later—in the shutting of the truck's doors, the rumbling of its engine, its wheels down the gravel road and away—before I'd fallen back to sleep.

And now it was light, and I was awake again. I left my cabin, hurried through the cold to the tub, where I let the hot water run and run, stripped off my pajamas, and stepped in. I soaked there as the fog hung heavy in the sky and the steam rose around.

I was lonelier than ever.

Eventually, I wrapped myself in my robe and returned to my room to build a fire. I had become used to the stacking of logs and twigs. The crunch of the newsprint, the strike of the match. I felt myself warm again, little by little, and then I looked at the clock and found it was not even ten in the morning. All the hours of the day stretched before me. Billy and Liz would be at the market. Terry and Julia had taken everyone else to town. I would need something to occupy myself.

I cooked a meal in the quiet kitchen and decided to call Karen. She'd been a constant for so long—the person I knew I could rely on—so it felt strange to have gone that many days without hearing her voice.

"Tell me *everything*," she said when she answered.

For a few minutes, as I told her about Lee and our

lessons, the house and the animals, the high schoolers and the children, I was less alone.

"How are Terry and Julia?"

"They're nice. They don't draw a lot of attention to themselves, I guess. They just make sure we all know our jobs and that the days move according to schedule."

"I can't remember if I told you, but they asked a *lot* of questions. They seemed intense."

I found that strange. "What kind of questions?"

"I can't remember exactly . . . Oh! I know. It was Terry. He said, 'Tell me about her resilience. Would you describe her as a *strong* person?' No one had ever asked that about one of my kids."

"What did you tell him?"

"I told him that after your mom and that man pulled you out of school, kept you in seclusion like that for a full *year*, you returned to school and made honor roll, and continued to make it every semester. They were clearly looking for exceptional people, so I told them the truth: that you are exceptional, you are resilient, you are amazing."

At first, I couldn't speak. I'd never heard anyone use those words to describe me. "Thank you," I managed to say.

"And is the farm . . . ?"

"Is it what?" I asked.

"I don't even know what to ask! Just—is it as wonderful as we hoped?"

"It is," I said.

I left it at that, and Karen assumed what she wanted—that all was good, all was safe. And maybe it was. I don't know what kept me from telling her everything, only that it seemed better to keep it to myself.

I promised to call her again soon and then I washed my breakfast dishes and headed to the schoolhouse.

It took me two hours just to empty the supply closet of its papers and costumes, old books and folders stuffed with lesson plans, faded paintings and collages and collections of protractors and rulers and calculators. There were baskets of buttons and boxes of thread and tubes of paint so old they were rock hard. I sorted all of it into piles across the room. I wheeled the garbage can from the side of the house and stuffed it with what could not be salvaged. I gathered questionable items into a basket for Terry to go through. Even then, when I looked across the schoolhouse to gauge my progress it was as though a hurricane had swept through. They could arrive back at any moment and find it this way. But all I could do was keep going.

In a far back corner of the closet I found a record player and a box of records. I opened the lid, expecting music, but what I found instead were educational recordings, what seemed to be lectures by experts on various subjects. I was disappointed at first—I'll admit it. I had imagined finding something soulful to get lost in. But I wiped the dust off the player anyway and pulled a record from its sleeve at random.

A crackle. A voice. *"Welcome to Ocean Explorations, an Introduction to Oceanography, produced by National Geographic."* Suddenly, I was no longer alone. As the narrator spoke of ocean currents and plate tectonics, I began to find order. Baskets and boxes once haphazardly filled were now empty, so I sorted and gathered and filled them again, lining them up neatly on the closet shelves. The record spun and taught me a new vocabulary—*upwelling, limnology, abyssal plains*—while I collected dozens of once-stray colored pencils, sharpened them, and tied them up in twine: a complete set now. The costumes I smoothed and hung from hangers on a rolling rack that had been impossible to access before. Sorting them gave me a glimpse into the past. They had performed *The Wizard of Oz* and *Alice in Wonderland*—those were the easiest to identify. Some of the costumes were meant to look medieval, while others had bell bottoms and fringe or African motifs. They had been forgotten for so long. They could have become mildewed and moth-eaten, but they had not.

I thought of the children who had worn them. I wondered if they'd really joined the family, as the article had said. If they had happy memories of this schoolhouse, if they returned for holidays and made themselves at home here. I was so lost in thought—my palms smoothing a furry little lion costume with a giant mane of brown yarn—when the record stopped. The needle lifted and moved to the side and the quiet that followed startled me.

The room felt suddenly chilly, as though the cold and silence had been there all along, lurking under the lecture and my busy movements, briefly obscured by my sense of purpose.

A shadow streaked across a wall. I held perfectly still, bracing for a memory to take me over. Wondering what would happen this time, after it was finished.

But no memory came.

I thought of Lee's face and his fear, that first day of lessons. And then I thought of his careful penmanship and the equations that finally made sense. Of how we moved on from it, safe in the schoolhouse.

Maybe the shadow was only my imagination.

I told myself that it was so.

I turned the record over and continued with my work until the room was neat again, with rows of clear tables and a closet that invited learning and play. I did it all without looking at the window. I did it with the record player's volume cranked as high as it would go.

By the time the third album had ended, I had finished labeling the shelves. I sat in the clean room, reading an old hardcover collection of Grimm's fairy tales, listening for the vans approaching from the road. Finally, I heard wheels on gravel, the groan of the gate.

I met them outside on the edge of the field. The children spilled out happily from one van and then the other. Lee gave me a quick, tight hug and then chased after the others to the house, where the high schoolers were going to prepare a snack. Terry and Julia greeted me with smiles. I led them to the schoolhouse and when I opened the closet, hope thrummed through me. *I am good,* I told myself. Here was proof on the shelves, in the three-inch spaces between each basket, in each carefully written label.

Would they see it?

I turned around. "I wanted to show you, in case you want anything arranged differently," I said, and hoped for their praise.

"Well, now look at this," Terry said. But Julia cocked her head, and soon Terry's brow furrowed. He started to speak and then paused. "*This* is how you spent your day?" he finally asked.

I nodded.

"This is your day off, Mila," Julia said. "Next time, go on a hike. Lie on the grass. Read a book or play the piano or stay in bed and do nothing. You don't need to have anything to show for your Sundays. Your Sundays are your own."

"Oh," I said. I tried to breathe. "Okay."

I was back at Jonathan and Amy's, scrubbing their sink

white, until Terry put his hand on my shoulder and said, "Mila, thank you. This is a huge weight off my mind, such a big help."

"Yes," Julia said, her voice softer, linking her arm through mine. "It's never looked so good in here. All these costumes—I'd forgotten about so many of them."

And then we walked across the field, Terry and me and Julia. Together, we stepped into their bright house.

That afternoon, I met Dr. Cole for the first time. He knocked twice at the kitchen door and stepped in with his black medical bag. "Time for checkups, everyone!" he boomed from the doorway.

Terry's voice called out from his bedroom: "Is that my brother?"

"The very one!" Dr. Cole called back.

Terry appeared in the kitchen and the two men embraced.

"Who wants the first checkup?" Dr. Cole asked. Ever eager, Lee's hand shot up.

They retreated to Terry and Julia's room and closed the door behind them. The dishes from the afternoon snack were stacked in the sink, so I got to washing and Julia soon joined me.

"Dr. Cole is one of our closest friends," she told me, dish towel over her shoulder. "He and Terry met in college, freshman year. Never let each other go."

Carefully, I handed Julia a large, wet platter. As she toweled it dry, she asked, "When was your last physical?"

"Just a few months ago."

She nodded. "And do you have any prescriptions you need filled? Any concerns, or matters you need checked on?"

"No."

"Some of our kids have chronic issues, so Dr. Cole comes by every few months for them, and we do regular yearly checkups for the others. Next year you can get your annual exam from Dr. Cole if you'd like. Or, a lot of our girls have preferred a female doctor. Dr. Harris in town is good. Tell me if you ever need an appointment and I'll set one up."

"Okay," I told her.

"For anything at all," she added.

"Thank you."

She finished stacking the clean plates and leaned against the sink, watching me. Was she waiting for me to say something? Before I could think of what, she said, "No more thank-yous. Not for things like this."

Just then, Lee burst out of the bedroom. His feet pounded through the living room to the doorway of the kitchen, where he stopped still, grinning. Julia and I paused our washing to take in the sight of his rumpled brown hair, his uneven front teeth—one large one, one gap with a new permanent tooth coming in. So proud of himself, so happy. He strode up to us.

"Well. How did it go?" Julia asked.

"I grew three-quarters of an inch!"

I sat on a kitchen chair so that I could be eye to eye with him.

"So much!" I said. "Soon you'll be up to the ceiling."

He threw his head back and laughed. "And . . . I'm perfectly healthy."

Julia widened her eyes. "No wheezing?"

"Nope."

"I'm so glad," she said.

Later, when the exams were over and Dr. Cole came out of the room, he spotted me and extended his hand. "You must be the new Samantha," he said.

What passed over my face? I didn't know I was so transparent, but his eyes widened and he shook his head. "What a strange thing to come out of my mouth. Tell me your name, my friend. I'm eager to know you."

"Mila," I said.

"Lovely name. And you're Lee's new teacher, correct?"

"Yes," I said. "Just like Samantha." I didn't want to be so sensitive. I tried to say it teasingly, but it came out bitter.

IN *TEACHING SCHOOL: A Handbook to Education on The Farm*, Terry and Julia wrote that if students can't focus it's best to work with their energy, to be spontaneous and flexible, to meet them where they are. So, one morning when Lee fidgeted all through the math lesson, I said, "Buddy. Your legs look like they want to move."

He grinned. "They do! They're saying, 'Please, please'!"

The field called to me through the window, wide and green and welcoming.

"How fast can they move?" I asked him. "Can they move faster than *my* legs?"

"Maybe," he said shyly.

"Let's race!"

So we rushed through the door and out onto the green, counted to three, and took off. I thought I would be faster. I was so much taller than Lee, after all. But he shot out ahead of me and kept his lead until we collapsed, panting, at the far edge of the field.

We raced again and again—he beat me each time—until we were both tired, lying on the grass.

"Lee," I said when we had caught our breath. "Do you know any fairy tales?"

"Sure," he said. "Plenty."

"I was thinking. Maybe we should make up fairy tales of our own, from our own lives."

"Like how?" he asked.

"We take things that happened to us, but we make them different."

"Okay," he said. "You go first. I think I almost understand."

"All right," I said, the cold, still-damp ground beneath me. I closed my eyes and I could just make out the sound of waves crashing. I opened them again to a flock of white birds passing soundlessly above. And then I was ready.

"Once there was a girl who was raised without a father, until her mother fell in love with a wolf."

Lee turned. I could feel him watching me. I thought of what to say next.

"She took her daughter to a wild place, for what wolf ever lived between walls? Her mother said, 'You must call him father. See how gentle he is?' and the wolf showed them his sharp smile. He growled and the mother said, 'Hear how kind he is? See how he loves us?' and he tore out the girl's heart with his teeth."

Lee sat up, quick.

"Oh, buddy," I said. "I'm sorry. Was it too scary?"

He pressed his hands together. Set them in his lap. Pressed them together again.

"No, I'm not scared," he said.

"I'll stop, though. I know it wasn't a very good story."

"No," he said. "It was really good. You can keep going. How does it end?"

I shook my head. I couldn't tell him. I had been thinking too much of myself, not nearly enough about him.

"Here," I said. "Let me tell you a better one. A happier one."

He nodded.

"I'll get all that badness out of your head."

Again, he pressed his palms together. "Thank you," he whispered.

I almost cried, seeing how I'd scared him. I would need to be more careful. "Okay. This one takes place before all of that."

Lee lay back down in the grass.

"Once, my mother was a girl of fifteen."

"Like Emma."

"Like Emma," I agreed.

"Sorry for interrupting."

I rolled onto my side and smoothed his hair. I did it the way a mother might, if he still had a mother. I said, "Once, my mother was a girl of fifteen. Just like our very own Emma.

She met a boy at a party, and soon she found out that she was . . . going to have a baby."

"*You?*"

"Me," I said. "Yes. They didn't *mean* for it to happen, but sometimes people make mistakes. She knew she wanted to have me, but she didn't know if the boy should be my father.

"She decided to give him three tests. If he passed them all, the answer would be yes.

"She called him up to see if he wanted to go to the movies, and he did. He drove to her house, wearing clean clothes, and knocked on her front door instead of waiting outside. That was the first test, and he passed it.

"When it was time to buy tickets, she said, 'I invited you to the movies, so I'm paying.' The boy put his wallet away and smiled and thanked her. That was the second test, and he passed it, too.

"Once the lights went dark in the theater, the boy kissed her. She kissed him back, but then turned to the screen when the movie started. He put his hands on her. 'Let's watch the movie,' she said. She already knew what his hands on her body felt like. She needed to learn other things about him.

"When the movie was almost over, she knew it was time for the third and final test. She found his hand in the dark and squeezed it. She wanted to know—*Was this boy patient?* But instead of squeezing back, his hand sat limp in hers as punishment. And so, after the movie was over, she said goodbye and never saw him again."

"Then what happened?"

"Her daughter was born and raised by her mother and her grammy and grandpa. She grew to be a girl, and they were mostly happy, most of the time. Life was simple and good."

"And then what?"

But I couldn't tell him the rest, even as it unspooled in my mind. I looked up at the sky and let the story continue, but only silently now, only for myself.

My mother met a man who lived in a skeleton house, cold enough in wintertime that he spent the nights drinking coffee at the diner where she worked. Night after night, she refilled his coffee cup. They found places to be alone together, did the things people do when they are falling in love. She invited him home to meet her family. In he walked, tall and strong in a green flannel shirt meant to accentuate his eyes. He smiled and flattered, but my grandparents saw something in him that felt dirty and dangerous, and they told my mother not to bring him back.

So she went to him instead. And at home she argued with my grandparents behind closed doors late at night. Their voices grew louder, their silences sharper, until one day she packed her things and mine, and took me away to a house with tarps for walls and the sky for a ceiling and a man who would be our undoing.

I was thirteen years old.

But, of course, I would not tell Lee all of that. I knew enough to be careful with him now.

"The end," I said. "Your turn. But only if you want to."

He looked across the field, out past the bluffs. "Once upon a time there was a boy and he was scared," he said, talking fast. "He was scared because his mother turned into a monster. And he wanted to tell his dad about it, but his dad was a monster, too. So he hid for a long time. It was dark. No one found him and he fell asleep."

Oh, Lee. I placed my hand on his back, between his shoulder blades. I would have carried all his pain for him if I could.

"How does it end?" I asked him.

"One day some people found him, with flashlights and badges, and they took him from one place to another place, until he ended up here. I mean, until he ended up in a pretty white house with a lot of nice people. And none of them were monsters. And he lived happily ever after. The end."

My eyes stung but I blinked the tears back, glad he wasn't looking.

"Did I do it right?" he asked.

"Yes," I told him. "*Yes.* You did it right." I knew it was

fast—we had known each other only for a very short time—but love for him swelled in my chest. I thought I could save us both. So I said, "Lee, I've been thinking. *Maybe* . . . when you feel the way you do sometimes. When you get scared in your chest and your stomach, you could try to invite what scares you *in*. Pay attention to it. Let it play back in your memory. I'm only now understanding it myself, but I think we have to face the things that scare us in order to move on from them. It might be the only way to stop being afraid."

He turned to his side to look at me.

"Do you understand?" I asked.

"I don't know," he said. "I think so."

And then Julia was crossing the field toward us, on her way to announce the end of school. She hovered above— employer, adoptive mother, giver of our happy endings— white haired and beaming.

"School time is over." She rang the bell and the three of us laughed.

"Want to go in for a snack?" Lee asked me.

"You go ahead," I told him. "I'm going to work in the schoolhouse. I'll see you in a little while."

Back in the schoolhouse, I thought of what I might do to hold Lee's attention the next week. We couldn't spend every day racing and telling fairy tales. We could try our math lesson standing up, away from the small desk. We could make a game out of it, with movements and prizes. I planned it all out. And then I spent some time with the shelf of novels, reading chapters from a few of them, deciding which one we should read next.

When I was finished, I closed up the schoolhouse and headed to my room.

I was nearing Liz's cabin when I heard something. I thought it might be a cat at first, or another kind of animal. I waited quietly, and then there came a deeper sound, and I realized what it was. Billy and Liz were in there, together, the curtain closed, the door shut. I heard her moan. Not a cat at all.

I took a step closer, as quietly as I could. I didn't mean to listen—not really—but I also didn't want them to hear me there on the path and know I had heard *them*. I was so close, only a foot away, and the cabins were so old and simple that I could hear the bedsprings groan up and down. I couldn't help myself—I imagined their position, imagined him moving inside her, imagined her hips and breasts and the looks on their faces. My knees went weak. They were louder now—I could hear them breathing hard, the springs moving faster, so I hurried toward my own room.

I took off my shoes at the door and climbed into my bed, suddenly hollowed out. I had known that first morning heading to the shower that they might have been together.

Every night, when they walked into one cabin or another, they weren't hiding anything. But still—I hadn't known for sure that it was something more than friendship, and knowing for certain now left me feeling foolish.

And yet, I couldn't get the sounds out of my head, nor the vision of them I'd created. I didn't *want* to get them out.

Was it wrong to think of Billy and Liz this way? Was it wrong to imagine them as I slid down my jeans, as I made myself moan the way they'd made each other?

I turned my head to the pillow, not wanting to be heard. Outside, it was daylight still, and Billy and Liz were naked in her cabin, and Julia was tending to her flowers, and Terry was most likely warming the oven for dinner. Maybe the little ones were playing ring-around-the-rosy. Maybe a flock of birds flew overhead. Maybe the ghosts were waking up. But I was alone in my tiny cabin. Alone in the rise and the shudder.

Alone in the quiet after.

That evening, I paused just outside the door of the main house. In the soft pink light, the field glowed a deep green. Rays of sunlight shone through clouds. I heard voices inside, lively and relaxed with the start of the weekend.

As soon as I entered, Billy touched my arm. "Mila, hey. I want to teach you to make butter. Interested?"

"Yes," I said.

"After, we can slice the loaves together. I'll show you all my tricks," Liz said, an uncommon ease about her. She leaned a hip against the cabinet and smiled.

"Sounds good," I answered.

"First," Billy said, "grab the bottle of cream from the refrigerator."

I did as he told me to, grateful for the blast of cold on my face. When I turned back, Liz was watching me.

"Something's up," she said.

"No," I said. "Just . . . I spent a while lesson planning. Then I took a nap. I'm just a little out of it, I guess."

"Hmm," she said.

We were only three people, standing in the kitchen, I told myself. It didn't need to be complicated.

To Billy, I said, "What's next?"

"You pour it into a mason jar, make sure the lid's on tight. And then you shake. *Forever*."

I laughed. "It sounds like you just want me to do the work." And they both laughed along with me.

Liz hopped up onto the counter, her bare feet dangling. "She's figured you out, Billy."

"No, but it's so *satisfying*. It starts out liquid and turns into *butter*. It's a *miracle*." His words were hyperbolic, but I could tell that he meant them. Liz rolled her eyes.

I shook the bottle until my arm got sore, then I switched hands and shook again. After a few minutes Liz offered to take a turn. I handed her the jar and noticed the gold chain around her wrist again, delicate but substantial.

"Your bracelet's so pretty."

"Thanks. Terry and Julia gave it to me." She didn't meet my eye when she said it, and then she was shaking the cream, fast.

"Be sure to give it to Mila before it's too late," Billy said. She did, and I experienced the moment he had described: One second I was shaking a liquid and the next it thumped in the jar.

"Open it up," he told me. "See the wet stuff? That's buttermilk."

"So cool."

"And now we take out the butter and strain it through a cheesecloth—to get the rest of the buttermilk out. After that comes my favorite part: stirring in the salt. *So* much salt. Way more than you think you need."

How simple, I thought. *How easy, all of it.* Being there with them. Learning the simple tricks of slicing the loaves—a sharp serrated knife; a firm hold; a sawing motion, back and forth rather than downward. Watching Billy scoop spoonfuls of gray sea salt and stir them into the butter.

"Hey," I said as he closed up the box of salt. "Your bracelet . . . it's the same as Liz's."

"Oh," he said. "Yeah."

"Terry and Julia?" I asked.

"Terry and Julia," he said. He glanced at Liz. They both looked sad and I didn't know why.

Liz reached for the bell that hung in the kitchen and rang it. Everyone came pouring in and took places around the table. Terry opened the oven door to take out the frittatas he'd cooked: egg and potato for the picky eaters, herb and goat cheese and mushroom for the rest of us. I slid onto a bench beside Lee.

Little Blanca climbed up next me.

"Hi, there," I said to her.

"I want bread."

"Bread coming up." I set a slice onto her plate.

She reached her arms out for the butter, and I was relieved to see her wrists were bare, that not everyone had these gifts but me. I spread the fresh butter on her slice, but as I looked at her happy face, I caught a flash of a gold necklace below it.

"Thank you," she said with her mouth full.

"Sure."

Across from me, Hunter dished himself a serving of salad with a gold-braceleted hand. Emma wore stacks of bangles on her wrists. Her neck was bare. But when she moved to tuck her hair behind her ear, I saw a gold band on her right hand—thin, simple—and I knew. Jackson's necklace was tucked into their shirt, but I could see a hint of it.

A necklace for Darius. A bracelet for James. On Mackenzie, a ring just like Emma's.

Finally, I let my gaze shift to Lee. *Not him, too,* I hoped. And no—not him. I knew him well enough already, the slenderness of his wrists, the curve of his neck, the bareness of his fingers. So, it was Lee and me, then. The only two not yet officially one of them. I didn't know what to make of it. Lee had been here for a long time.

"Goat cheese and herb?" Terry asked from over my shoulder. I nodded yes.

"And you, young man?"

"I'll try that one, too. Since Mila's having it," Lee said.

I was grateful for Lee by my side. Now that I knew about the chains and rings, I felt the nakedness of my wrists and neck and fingers. Even though I told myself I was fine, that I had only been there for a few weeks, I was still ashamed. I found myself placing my hands in my lap whenever I wasn't using my fork and knife. I let my hair fall over my neck to hide its bareness.

"Mila made the butter tonight," Liz said.

"You did!" Julia said. "It's delicious."

I nodded, but wanted their eyes off me, however friendly their expressions, however innocuous their attention. All I could think was, *Look at Mila. The one who knows nothing. The one who isn't one of us.* I felt my hand take hold of Lee's under the table. He smiled at me and squeezed mine back. At least I had him. At least there were two of us.

Later, after we'd cleared the dishes and the high schoolers had taken their stations to wash and dry, I found Lee in the living room, looking out the dark window.

"What's up, buddy?" I asked him.

"It's my ghost. He's making mean faces."

As soon as I looked toward the window, the ghost turned and darted away. It was much smaller than Lee was. If it were human, it could not have been more than five years old.

"Lee, what do you mean, *your* ghost?"

He turned to me, as though surprised. As though he hadn't realized he was speaking to me at all. "Oh," he said. "It just . . . follows me. I think it likes me."

I rumpled his hair. "Well, I don't blame it. Who wouldn't like *you*?"

He tried to smile, but he was blinking tears away, turning his face so that I couldn't see it.

"Can I read you a story?" I offered, but he shook his head.

"I think I'll just go to sleep."

"Okay."

He gave me a quick hug and climbed the stairs.

———————

A few days later, Lee and I were alone in the schoolhouse. Billy had the little ones out on a nature walk and, because Terry and Julia were away meeting Ruby and Diamond—the twins who would soon be coming to live with us—the high schoolers had persuaded Liz to hold class in the living room.

We'd finished math and reading and now it was time for art. Together, we were learning about one-point perspective from a book.

Next to each other at the big table, with large sheets of paper and chalk pastels, Lee drew a room with ceilings and walls and a floor. Every line was careful. And *I* was being careful, too. I'd been thinking of our fairy tales in the field, about the ghost in the window, about the way he withdrew when he was afraid. I had a plan to help him, and it required me to be brave.

So I drew a street, flanked by sidewalks, growing narrow in the distance. I felt a tremble in my hand and paused to read aloud from the book about depth and scale.

And then I said, "Let's keep drawing. Fill up your room."

Lee added a table and chairs and light fixtures. Books and plants and people. And I added my own details. Telephone wires with birds perched atop them. A window, through which a father and son worked a puzzle.

I was drawing the view from the skeleton house.

My hand trembled—I couldn't stop it this time—and

the pastel slipped from my fingers. I feared the remembering would swallow me whole. But Lee pushed out from the table, dipped low and resurfaced with my pastel. I took it from his hand as he scooted back in.

"Your drawing looks so good," he said. "Keep going."

He was adding color to his own now, making careful marks and blending them with his finger. I almost cried as I watched him. How easily he had brought me back. How safe and strong I felt with him next to me.

"Do you want to know something?" I asked, roughing out a figure on my paper, confident now.

Eagerly, Lee nodded.

"All right. But first a question. Had you seen ghosts before coming here?"

"No."

"Well, I had. Just one of them. She was my very *own* ghost and I knew her name and everything."

"Her *name*?"

"Yes."

"Wow," he said. We worked for a little while in silence before he asked, "Will you tell it to me?"

"Sure. Her name was Lorna. She haunted the street corner below the place where I lived."

"What did she do?"

I was adding her details—her nightgown, her eyes.

"She mostly stood around. She held different things in her hands. She stared in my direction."

"She didn't do much, then."

"Not very much, no."

My drawing was finished. There was Lorna, my ghost, holding her plastic flowers. I had drawn her as well as I knew how. She was just marks on a page; nothing more.

Lee shivered.

"It scares you?" I asked.

"No," he said quickly.

"It's okay to be afraid," I said. Now was my moment. I thought carefully, took in a breath, and began. "I spent a really long time, years and years, trying to forget about everything that scared me. And then, my first day here, I sat next to you—right in this chair—and told you a secret from my past."

"Your ear piercings," Lee said.

"Yes." He was leaning toward me, a worried line between his brow. "The thing is," I continued, "I'm learning that it's *good* to think about what scares you. To bring it into the light. Even to hold it in your hands, if you can, and feel how it can't hurt you anymore. To think of it and say, 'I am not afraid.'"

Lee watched me so closely. I could tell he understood.

"It takes away its power, to look at it that way."

"So I should look at my ghost?"

"Yes," I said. "And other things, too. Here, I'll show you." I drew in a breath, felt the racing of my heart. "I was living in a bad place when I saw Lorna. It was a hard time. It was a bad time. It was . . ." I closed my eyes, let out a slow breath. "At first, I was frightened by the sight of her, but the longer I looked, the less frightening she became. And even though everything else was hard, everything else was *bad*, she was only herself, and I found comfort in her."

I felt calmer, breathed easily again. "Do you understand what I'm saying, Lee?"

"I think so," he said. "It's just . . ."

"What is it, Lee?"

"Nothing," he said.

I placed my hand on his shoulder and smiled. "You can tell me."

"It's just . . . ," he said. "It was never this way with Samantha."

"What way?"

"Samantha never told me about her life. We just did lessons."

My cheeks burned. A vision of Samantha came to me—a confident girl, an easier, better girl than me—sitting with Lee and helping him learn. He probably trusted her enough to make mistakes. But what was he trying to tell me? Was I sharing too much?

I was only trying to help him. I was helping him the best that I could. I took my hand off his shoulder. I shifted my body away. I felt my posture stiffen and I tried to think of something to say but couldn't.

"I don't mean it in a bad way," he said.

Could that be true?

"Oh no," Lee said. "I think I said it wrong. She never *cared* that much about me. That's what I was trying to say."

I turned my gaze to his—his face upturned, his wide brown eyes confused, concerned. I could have cried with relief. It was all a misunderstanding. I was being too sensitive again.

I exhaled, my body softened. "Oh, Lee," I said. "It's *fine*."

"I'm sorry if you thought . . ."

"We don't have to say another word about it."

After dinner that night, Julia asked me to go with her to the flower tunnel. "I need to teach you more of the names," she said "We won't have long before it gets too dark, but I have to cut stems for a friend's dinner party in town. Might as well teach you something as I do." We stepped in, all soft light and color and fragrance. "Do you remember the names of these?" she asked, pointing to the bruise-colored flowers I had loved from before.

"Anemones," I answered.

"Good girl."

She showed me the heirloom chrysanthemums, the Henriette dahlias, the zinnias. "That's all I'll ask you to remember for today," she said. "A few at a time, over time, does the trick. Now help me cut. The best harvesting times are very early morning and night. The heat of the day shocks them, shortens their life. We want them to last several days cut, if not even longer."

A pair of sharp scissors in my hand, I cut where she told me to and set the stems in buckets of water. We worked quietly for a little while, and then I confessed, "I read about you in the newspaper."

"When?"

"Before I came. An article from a long time ago."

"They like to romanticize us," she said.

"Like a fairy tale," I said softly, more to myself than to her. But she heard me and agreed.

"Very much like a fairy tale. Yes. Fairy tales are full of orphans and mistreated children. The movies make them romantic, but the original stories are not. And there's nothing romantic about giving a home to young people who need one. It's a necessity, and it's something Terry and I like and are good at."

"So, a new fairy tale," I said. "Except with ghosts."

She brushed a white curl off her forehead with a gloved hand and paused. "Are there no ghosts in fairy tales?" We thought and thought and couldn't think of any. Not in Snow

White or Cinderella. Not in Sleeping Beauty or Rumpel-stiltskin or Rapunzel. Not in the Twelve Dancing Princesses or The Goose Girl.

Night was falling. Soon it would be too dark for us to keep cutting and filling the buckets.

Julia wiped her hands on her work apron. "So, now we load up the wheelbarrow and take them to the cooler. They'll chill overnight and then, first thing in the morning, I'll arrange the bouquets."

Together, we carried the buckets of flowers to the worn wheelbarrow, all wood and rusted metal, and fit in as many as we could. I followed her around the tunnel and to the back of the house, until we reached a shed that housed a walk-in refrigerator. After setting the buckets on the shelves, we made another trip with the rest of the flowers, and then we were finished.

We closed up the shed and headed back toward the house. I took everything in as we walked together. The cold, wet air. Two ghost children on the green, pretending to have a picnic. The darkness and sky and the moon above the rocks.

"Coming back in?" Julia asked me at the side door.

I shook my head.

"Good night then, Mila," she said.

"Good night."

Summer was fading, the days still warm but the nights colder, and while the sky had been clear only a moment ago, a fog settled as I made my way to the other end of the field. I wished I had thought to take a lantern, but I made it to the barn door and let myself in. I felt across the inside wall for the switch and found it—but stopped before turning it on. What would the others think if they saw the schoolhouse suddenly bright? I wanted to be left alone there, without anyone checking on me. So I waited for my eyes to adjust before making my way to the closet, where beeswax taper candles rested in a basket, their holders in another. By the woodstove was a box of matches. I struck one and lit the candle, set it on the table.

I sat alone in the quiet.

"The common man pays for more than electricity and gas and water," Blake told us one morning.

The summer was over but they hadn't sent me back to school. Both of us—my mother and I—had to unlearn what we'd spent our lives learning. Blake would help us. He taught us the new lessons late at night, in the mornings when my mother returned from work with sore feet and tired eyes, around the fire and inside the frame of his skeleton house.

"The common man pays for the internet," he went on. "He pays for cable, for Christ's sake! Because he needs more and more and more! Like anyone could watch one hundred channels. What good is a life if you live it like that? Glued to a lightbox showing you pictures. Telling you when to laugh and what to fear. The common man lives this way because he has lost the intuition of our ancestors. All you need in order to live is *this*." He took two fingers and pressed them to my mother's wrist. Waited, waited, and then nodded.

He let go and took my wrist in his rough hand. "Have you ever taken your pulse, Mila?" he asked me. His voice was lower now, as though these words were for me only.

"I can't remember," I said.

"I feel it," he whispered. "*Boom. Boom. Boom.* Here. You try."

I pressed my fingers where his had been but I couldn't feel anything.

"Keep trying," he told me.

I moved them. I pressed harder. When I looked up, his green eyes were watching me. "It's all right, sweet girl," he said in a kind voice. "You'll find it. I can see it in you—the intuition is not too far buried."

"What about me?" My mother laughed. "Am I a lost cause?" It sounded like a joke but I knew better.

"Oh, Miriam," Blake said, and looked away.

"What?" she asked.

"I shouldn't say it," he said. "Let's not worry."

"You shouldn't say *what*?"

"It's just . . ." He turned his face to the sky. He looked at her and squeezed his eyes shut as though what he was thinking pained him. "You have a deficit," he finally said. "But let's just hope for the best."

"What do you mean, 'a deficit'?"

"We don't have to discuss this, love."

"Blake," she said. "I want to know."

"Well, here it is. It is a sad truth, but the science can't be argued with. Teenagers—not just you, Mila, but all of them—they have trouble regulating their emotional responses. This is about the amygdala, you see, which is part of the brain, and how it interacts with the frontal cortex. It's about the balance between emotion and judgment. That's where the intuition lies. You need to find the balance. But when a girl gets pregnant as a teenager, when her amygdala isn't yet fully formed, the pregnancy hormones take over during the most crucial years, the *formative* years."

"Then what?" my mother asked. I could feel her worry, could see it in her face.

"Then you may never develop the intuition you need to exist as an independent person in the world. You've never been one, Miriam. It isn't your fault. It's the cards you were dealt. When you first told me that you had a daughter, I considered calling it off. I spent many a sleepless night thinking it over. Not because of the responsibility of a stepchild—which is not insignificant—but because of the deficits that teen motherhood causes."

My mother sat very still, her hands cupped in her lap.

I said, "But don't they kind of have to grow up faster?"

"Common misconception," he said. "I mean, sure, some of them drop out of high school and enter the workforce sooner. But is that growing up? Hardly. It's a chemical problem. The pregnancy hormones and adolescent hormones. They clash. It has all kinds of side effects in the brain. Really, Miriam. Sometimes it may feel like I'm hard on you but it's a miracle that you're doing as well as you are."

My mother seemed hopeful then. He put his arm around her and she turned her face to his chest. I saw her finding comfort in it. I was cold and confused and I wanted to be the one she was breathing in. I wanted her to hold me all night like she had when I was little.

"You two," Blake said. "You're lucky to be here with me. I'll look out for you. And this is a special property. A special place. You know, a long time ago, it was oceanfront property. Hell, with global warming going the way it is, it's bound to be oceanfront property again one day."

My mother didn't say anything. Her head was still nestled in his chest. *Oceanfront?* I thought. It didn't seem possible. We were several towns in from the bay, let alone the ocean. I saw him looking at me. I didn't say anything.

A few days later, I stepped on something sharp. It cut through the thin sole of my shoe, into my foot.

A shell, right there, in the dirt.

Blake smiled.

"Don't doubt me, Mila," he said.

My body pulsed with energy as I left the schoolhouse. I could see clearly in the dark even without a lantern to guide me. When I inhaled, I tasted air and ocean and grass. I felt the softness of my sweater against my skin, the coldness of the night, the thump of my feet against the ground. My heartbeat was its own music.

Ghosts glowed in the distance but I didn't mind them. I moved steadily forward, strides long and purposeful, past the main house to the garden and through it until I reached the rows of strawberries. The sky was clear, the moonlight bright enough that I could spot the berries hidden among the waxy leaves. Twist of stem, berry in my palm.

They tasted like sugar and the soil they came from. Soft between my teeth, and sweet. I held one in my mouth, lay on my back between the rows, let my body melt into the cold ground.

Tiny bright stars studded the black sky, more of them and brighter than I'd ever seen.

Boom, boom, boom beat my heart.

I was not afraid of anything.

Once I had eaten my fill and was headed back, a light shone through the thickening fog. A leap and a spin. The dancing ghost, still yards away but closer to me than she'd ever been. I stopped to watch her—we were miracles, all of us—but her light hurt my eyes and I had to turn away. Another figure, not glowing, leaned against the wall of the second cabin.

"Hey, Mila," he said as I neared him.

"Hey, Billy," I said, amazed by the clear lightness of my voice.

"You doing okay?" he asked.

"Yeah," I said.

"All right."

I lifted my hand as a gesture of departure, and he nodded and went inside. I walked straight to the bathroom to prepare for bed and then, finally, to my cabin door.

As soon as I let myself in, my exhilaration left me. In its place came an ache—from my hip to my ribs to my shoulder—an ache I remembered from sleeping on the hard floor of Blake's house. I felt a sting on my foot. Touched it and felt wetness between my fingers. Saw a half-moon of blood in the spot where Blake's shell had sliced me.

I went through the motions of building the fire. I pressed a tissue against my cut to blot the blood. I climbed, shivering, into bed. I rubbed my sore hip. I rubbed my shoulder. I closed my eyes and saw Blake. Wondered, again, whether his ghost had followed me here.

I searched for something of comfort, but not even the

moon was visible through the skylight, so thick was the fog. Tears dampened my pillow.

I wished Grammy was there to sing to me, to rub my back in circles like she used to.

"There's a somebody I'm longing to see," I sang to myself instead.

I remembered every word.

I sang until the song was over, and then I sang it again.

celebration

A KNOCK AT MY DOOR WOKE ME. It was morning, and as I eased myself out of bed I was surprised that the ache in my side remained even in daylight. I checked my foot—a dried speck of blood but nothing more. I didn't know what to make of it—didn't know what to feel.

Before unlatching and opening the door, I glanced at myself in the mirror and smoothed my hair, relieved to find I still looked like myself.

Lee was on my doorstep, smiling, a breakfast tray in his hand.

"Happy birthday!" he said. "You're a whole decade older than me now."

"And you've brought me breakfast in bed?"

"Julia sent me. She made you pancakes and bacon. And she sent a plate for me, too, but she said not to stay too long because sometimes people like quiet mornings on their birthdays." His smile widened. "*But*, I mean, it *is* Saturday. So if you don't want a quiet morning, I can stay as long as you want."

"Come in," I told him, laughing, and I barely felt the soreness anymore. I was full of light. Lee and me in my little cabin. "I'll warm it up in here," I said.

"We'll have an inside picnic."

"That sounds amazing!"

I piled the logs and crumpled the newspaper, smiling through all of it, and when I turned, Lee had set the tray on the rug by the bed. Two heaping plates and a small pitcher of syrup. Butter in a little dish. A glass of milk. A mug of coffee with cream.

I sat across from Lee on the rug. He was dressed in his pajamas and I was in my nightgown. The room smelled like maple, and the night before was gone.

"Would you like syrup, milady?" Lee asked in a formal, unidentifiable accent, holding the pitcher daintily between two fingers.

"Why yes, good sir," I said, and he poured, and we ate until our plates were empty, and I felt like a girl from a novel or a movie. I felt like a girl from a different time. And all the while I told myself, *Remember this feeling. How perfect this is. Remember Lee's sweet face and his proper manners. Remember the maple and the salt. Remember the warmth of the coffee in your mouth. The crackling of the fire, the glow of the room in the early morning when it's just you and Lee and the world is safe.*

"Julia told me I should let you relax. And that you don't

have to help with the harvest today. So I can go now and take these back and you can read or draw or just . . . do whatever!"

He stacked the plates and the silverware, set our cups back on the tray. I watched his expression of expectancy, could tell he was hoping I'd say something.

"Or . . . ," I said. "Maybe you could come back in a little while and we can go exploring."

He beamed. "Okay, if you're sure."

"I'm sure."

"Julia said to make sure you were sure."

"I'm sure that I'm sure. Let me get that door for you."

He slipped out, the tray clutched in his arms. "I'll be back soon!"

"I'll be here," I told him. Before I closed the door, I heard the rumble of the truck, saw Billy and Liz roll down the gravel drive toward the highway. Liz was driving. Billy saw me and waved from the passenger seat, and I waved back, feeling wistful in spite of my plan with Lee, wishing they would have at least invited me along to wherever they were going.

I thought of Billy and Liz again later that afternoon, when Lee and I had returned from a hike through the hills behind the farm and found the truck still gone.

"What do you want to do now?" Lee asked me. We were

sitting together in a patch of grass near the rows of vegetables, catching our breath. "We could draw or tell fairy tales again, if you want."

I felt a tightness in my throat. "No," I said. "I don't want to remember anything today. I just want to be here."

He took my hand. "I understand," he said.

I looked at our interlaced fingers, thought of the truck, driving away. "Lee, you don't have a ring or a bracelet or a necklace."

"I know. I want one."

"I want one too."

"How will we get them?"

"I don't know."

A bird arced in the sky. Tulip darted past us, after something, through the rows.

"This place . . . ," I said.

"Yeah," he said. And he rolled onto his back. I did the same. And it was Lee and me in the daylight, our bodies against the grass, not knowing what any of it meant.

The house was strangely quiet when I entered through the mudroom for dinner. But I sensed life, heard the faint sounds of breathing. Strung in the doorway between the kitchen and living room was a banner that spelled HAPPY BIRTHDAY, each letter stitched onto its own little flag. For the second time that day, joy sprung to my heart. I stepped under the sign and peeked around the corner.

There was everybody, huddled by the piano. Lee and Terry and Julia. Billy and Liz. Emma and Jackson and Hunter. Little Darius and Blanca and Mackenzie and James.

"Surprise!" they all shouted. The little ones cracked up laughing—I couldn't believe they'd held so still, been so quiet even for a few moments. Lee bounced up and down on his feet, a grin across his sweet face.

"Nineteen." Julia shook her head as though it were a monumental achievement, as though they'd known me all my life. When she stepped forward to hug me, I allowed myself to imagine—only very briefly, only while in her embrace—that Terry and Julia had an album of photographs of me, that I had lived in the main house when I was little, soaked in the upstairs tub, learned to read and set the table, grown up as they watched me.

And then she let me go.

"Thank you," I said to all of them. "I'm so lucky."

"*We're* lucky," Terry said. "Lucky to get to celebrate you."

Julia disappeared to the kitchen to set up the little ones at the table with bowls of soup and *Mary Poppins*. The rest of us waited in the living room and soon she returned carrying a tray of sparkling cider in champagne flutes. She handed one to each of us, and Terry said, "To Mila!" and we all clinked glasses. My face was hot with the attention, so I walked over to a corner where a collection of CDs was stacked on the built-in shelves. I didn't recognize the names on the cases. Soon, I felt someone near me. Liz.

"I can't believe you still have these things," she told Terry as she plucked a CD from a stack. "Look good?" she asked me.

I shrugged. "I don't know any of them. So, sure."

She laughed and handed it to Terry, who turned on the CD player and pressed some buttons. The disc disappeared into a slot. "We've never cared much about keeping up with the times," he said. "No reason to out here." The sound of a keyboard and a drum machine came through the speakers, followed by a woman's voice. Terry extended an arm to Julia and they began to dance. Lee joined and they made space for him between them.

I settled onto the sofa to watch. I expected Billy and Liz to dance, too, but instead they sat next to me. "Did you go to town?" I asked.

"Yeah," Billy said, brushing hair from his eyes.

"You didn't stay long."

"Of course not," Liz said. "We came back for *you.*" She bumped my shoulder with her own. My heart swelled with it—how familiar she was acting toward me. I didn't move away, kept my shoulder against hers. I pretended that it was casual, that it didn't mean so much to me.

"Hey," Billy said, leaning closer to me too. "You get

to come to market with us tomorrow. Terry told us this morning."

"*Oh*. I'm so glad." For two months, I had not traveled in a car. I hadn't been any farther than the beach across the highway. Soon, I would be out in the world again.

"I wish *we* could work the market," Hunter said. I'd been so focused on Billy and Liz that I hadn't realized he'd been listening. But when I looked, I saw that Emma and Jackson were watching us, too. "It would be way better than harvesting," he added.

Emma rolled her eyes. "Don't complain."

"I can complain if I want to."

"Okay, fine. Go ahead then," she said.

We talked about the crop for a while, about how the summer was turning to fall, and what would soon be growing instead of strawberries and tomatoes.

"Soon *all* we'll be eating is butternut squash," Jackson said, rolling their eyes.

"Don't forget kabocha and delicata," Hunter teased them.

"How could I?" Jackson said.

"Well, we have something more exciting than squash this afternoon," Julia said as a song finished playing. She nodded to Billy and Liz, who stood and went to the kitchen. They returned a few minutes later, Billy carrying a chocolate cake, my name written in the middle, adorned with white candles.

"Make a wish, Mila," he said.

"Yes," Julia said. "Make a wish. Wish for anything."

I wish I could be one of you, I thought. And then I blew out the candles. Billy cut thick slices while everyone lined up with plates. Liz brought out tea.

We settled again, all of us in new places across the living room. It felt like a dream, but the bright gray afternoon light shone through the windows and everything was clear: the cake crumbs on the plates, and the steam from the teapot Julia kept refilling. The books lining the wall on each side of the giant hearth, Lee sitting straight-backed in the center, and the stack of wood on the grate for when the cold came in. Jackson, Emma, and Hunter in a heap on the sofa; the little ones playing with clay while watching their movie—the faint sound of Mary Poppins singing. Billy sat cross-legged on the floor, leaning against the chair. Liz lounged on floor pillows across the room. Terry rocked in his wood rocking chair, and Julia moved about us all easily, gathering empty plates, checking on the children, making sure we were all warm and cared for.

"And now," Julia said, rising, "I think it's time for gifts."

Hope rushed over me. *A ring or a necklace or a bracelet of my own.* But Julia emerged from her room with two wrapped packages, both much too large, and I had to hide my disappointment.

"Open the big one first," Liz said, sitting up to watch me.

The package was heavier than I expected it to be. Carefully, I tore open the paper. I saw a suitcase of sorts, blue gray and old, with a handle and two metal buckles. I unlatched the buckles to see what was inside. "A record player!" I said. So then I knew what would be in the flat, square package. I tore off the paper, eager to see the record. It was Billie Holiday, singing Gershwin songs.

I didn't know what to say.

"Julia gave us some ideas," Billy said.

"I hope you like Billie Holiday," Liz said. "The record shop guy showed us like twenty options of records with those same songs, but she seemed like the coolest."

"She had the best name," Billy said. "Spells it weird, but still."

I laughed. I didn't know anything about Billie Holiday, but the songs were listed on the back and I recognized all their titles. Now I would have music in my cabin. Now it wouldn't be so quiet in there all the time.

"Thank you," I said to them.

"You're welcome," Julia said. "We're so glad to have you here."

"Especially me." Lee scrambled to his feet and gave me a hug, tight and quick, before going back to his place at the hearth.

"Let's listen," Billy said. "I want to hear what it sounds like."

"The needle's new," Liz told me. "The guy at the record store put it in for us."

I had gotten used to the record player in the schoolhouse, so I knew what to do. I slipped the record out of its sleeve and set it onto the player. I lowered the needle, and the record began to spin. Music crackled out. Her voice surprised me—it was not the smooth, crooning sound I'd heard as a child. But the words and the melodies were the same. Once the first song played through and the second began, I got used to the way she sounded. And I thought it made sense that I'd be listening to a different voice now, a rougher one. I was glad for the difference. There was no going back. Never again would I sit next to Grammy at the piano, positioning my fingers as she had. Grandpa would never again turn up the volume. Never ask me to dance. All of that was over. This is what I had now. The sun was lowering in the sky, so Julia lit the fire and the flame's crackle joined with the record's, and soon the room filled with warmth.

I allowed myself to believe I was one of them, then. That the celebration made it official. The cake and the gifts. This afternoon together. I sank into the easy chair and listened to the songs I knew by heart sung in a new voice, and felt that I belonged. *Mary Poppins* ended and the little ones joined us, showing off their clay sculptures, begging for their slices of cake. Billy brought out plates for each of them and lined them up on the coffee table. He tucked their napkins into their shirts and they ate with determination. All of us were there, in the room together. All of us were listening to the record, and feeling the warmth, and I thought the moment was perfect. It *was* perfect.

Until a movement outside made me turn to the window. A quick flash and then—*whack!*

Emma screamed. "Oh my *God*, what *was* that?"

"Something hit the window," Liz said. We stood up and put on our shoes, went outside to see. We gathered around it—Terry and Julia and Lee, Emma and Hunter and Jackson, Blanca and Darius and James and Mackenzie, Billy and Liz and me.

A bird.

Eyes forever open with a broken wing. Scattered feathers and a little yellow beak. A gray, dead thing at our feet.

"I'll dig a grave," Terry said.

I wanted a bird-ghost. Night fell and I returned to my cabin with the record under my arm, carrying the player by the handle, watching for a glowing, flying thing.

I wanted a kind of logic. A reason. An assurance that things worked the way they were supposed to. Creatures lived and they died and sometimes they returned in a different form. Sometimes they haunted the living, and sometimes they let us be.

I set the record player on my little writing table and

stretched out the hand that had carried it, rubbed at the indentations the handle had made. I plugged it in, slipped the record from its sleeve, and lowered the needle. Here was that piano again, that mournful, strange voice. I sat at the wooden chair and watched out the window.

That poor little bird. Still black eyes and a fragile, broken wing.

I wanted a bird-ghost. But it never appeared to me.

good things take time

MY ALARM CUT THROUGH THE DARK: five a.m. My first farmers' market morning.

I didn't bother building a fire. I brought my clothes with me to the shower and made quick work of the soap and shampoo—shivering all the while—and dressed quickly in jeans and a thermal shirt and a navy corduroy jacket Julia had chosen for me from the closet upstairs. It was worn and soft and I wondered how many interns had used it in these early morning hours to keep themselves warm as they headed to town. I laced up my boots and crossed the field, found the truck untouched since the night before. I could see the light on in the kitchen and Liz inside, brewing coffee. I was glad I wasn't late.

I headed to the refrigerator around back and made trips to and from the truck with the wheelbarrow of flowers. By the time I'd carried the last of the buckets, Billy was letting down the gate of the truck.

"Morning," he said.

"Morning," I said.

He hopped up into the truck bed and held out his hands. I passed him bucket after bucket, silently calling the flowers by name so I'd remember. *Heirloom chrysanthemums. Dahlias. Zinnias. Yarrow. Anemones. Icelandic poppies.*

The mudroom door opened and there was Liz, three thermoses in her hands. She saw how I'd moved all the buckets already.

"Thank God there are three of us now," she said, and I forgot all about the cold.

Billy surveyed the contents of the truck bed with his lantern. Strawberries and lettuces and summer squash. Tomatoes and basil. Buckets and buckets of flowers. Three wooden folding tables and some canvas tarps. A cashbox and two scales. "Looks like we're all set," he said.

He hopped down and dangled the keys toward Liz. "You or me?"

"You there, me on the way back?"

He nodded and got into the driver's seat. I didn't know what to do—whether Liz would want to sit next to Billy or whether she'd prefer to avoid the narrow middle seat.

"Go ahead," she told me. So I did. I pushed a first-aid kit under the seat to clear space for my feet and Liz climbed in after me. Billy, me, and Liz, our shoulders touching as I knew they would. She handed me a thermos for Billy and a thermos for me and shut the door. Billy started the engine and rolled down the drive. Liz jumped out to open the gate and then closed it behind us.

"It takes about forty-five minutes," she told me as Billy turned onto Highway One. She reached across my body to turn on some music. Out of the speakers came a man's voice, raspy and calm. He sang like he was tired, and Billy drove us up the coast as we sipped our coffees and the sun rose.

Mendocino greeted us with its tiny business district, its weathered fences and pristine bed-and-breakfasts, its narrow streets and wildflowers and bluffs overlooking crashing waves. Billy and Liz said hi to the other vendors as we passed them—some older farmers, a few people our age. "This is Mila," they said, over and over, and told me the vendors' names and what goods they were known for. We set up the tables and the tent cover, and then it was time to unload the truck. Out to the street and back, over and over, buckets and crates in our arms. We walked carefully, over the curb and through the market, but when we were almost finished Liz tripped over our neighbor's tent pole and fell, holding tight to her bucket of flowers. I set mine down and took the bucket from her so that she could stand.

"*Shit*. Are they okay?" she asked. Half of her shirt was soaked, but the flowers were unharmed.

"Yeah, they're fine," I said. "Are *you*?"

"Yeah." But she grimaced and tugged down one side of

her jeans. She'd scraped her hip. I remembered the first-aid kit from the truck, so I grabbed the keys from Billy and ran to get it. I came back to find her sitting on a folding chair with a bag of ice from the cheese stand. I showed her the kit. She nodded.

"Whenever you're ready," I told her.

"I'll just ice it for a couple more minutes first," she said.

Billy and I went to work setting up the table. It didn't take much to make it pretty. The flowers and produce were beautiful enough, but Julia had also tucked woven baskets into the crates, and twine to tie the flowers. Billy and I worked together, filling the baskets with bright red tomatoes, tying the basil into bunches and scattering them around, stacking yellow squashes and arranging the flowers into bouquets, small ones for ten dollars, larger for twenty.

I saw Liz set down her ice, so I returned to her and opened the box. I rubbed my hands with alcohol and looked at the scrape again, right along the sharp bone of her hip. It was deeper than I had realized, the skin bruising around it.

"Should we put alcohol on it?" I asked her. "I think we should, but it'll hurt."

"Yeah," she said. "Probably."

So I found gauze and wetted it.

"What was it, again?" I asked, eyes on the gauze, too shy to look at her face. "As you feel the pain begin . . . ?"

"Press it close and count to ten," she said.

I touched the gauze to the cut, felt her flinch.

"One . . . two . . . three . . . "—I removed the gauze and set it down—"four . . . five . . . six . . . "—tore open a bandage and covered the center with antiseptic—"seven . . . eight . . . nine . . . "—lined the bandage up and gently pressed it to her skin—"ten."

I snuck a look at her face. She narrowed her eyes and smiled.

I had impressed her.

"You can just watch at first," Liz said, when she took position behind the cashbox and scale. "And refill the tables whenever they look picked over. And then, if you want to, you can help us with the weighing and the money."

"It's as simple as it sounds," Billy said. "The trick is not to let the line intimidate you. Everyone can wait a few minutes for flowers. There's no rush."

Even before the market was officially open, a few people were waiting at our booth. Other vendors had flowers, too, but Julia's were different—rare and surprising and impossibly beautiful. I remembered Nick, on my first night at the farm, telling me that Julia was famous for them. I could see what he meant. While Liz and Billy rang up the first shoppers, I kept busy, replacing the purchased arrangements with new ones from the buckets behind the tables. I helped customers set strawberry cartons into their bags, place tomatoes in baskets. The time passed quickly with so much work to do, and throughout it all, I watched Billy and Liz as they worked. They made quick and friendly conversation, advising against storing flowers with fruit, explaining how to make the bouquets last through the week. They offered tips on cooking eggplant and commented on the weather— how warm and clear August had been this year. "Say hi to Julia and Terry," so many people said. "Will do," Liz said. "You got it," said Billy.

A couple hours in, when the line was still steady but no extra arrangements remained in buckets, Billy beckoned me over. "Ready to weigh?" he asked. I was. And it felt good—to think quickly that way, to take money and count change, to smile at the next stranger and say hello.

Once the market closed, we broke down the tables and folded the canvas. Liz and Billy traded our leftover produce for honey and wine and gray salt to bring back to the farm. Billy counted out our hourly wages from the cashbox and placed the bills in our palms. I hadn't even known to expect payment and felt a giddy freedom exploring the downtown with money in my pocket: the bookshop and the chocolate shop, the cafés and the toy store. I bought a novel—*Rebecca* by Daphne du Maurier. It was thick and moody and something in the description made me think of myself. And I also bought two tins of watercolors, two brushes, and two little notebooks of watercolor paper. One set for myself and one set for Lee.

There were plenty of art supplies at the farm, but I wanted something of my own. Something new, something that was only ever mine. And I thought Lee might want that, too.

"Dinner?" Billy asked, and Liz and I agreed. I followed them a couple blocks to a pub where the vendors from another farm were eating. We waved when we saw them, and they made space for us at their big table. They were just a little older than we were, and I could tell Billy and Liz had hung out with them before. We ate onion rings and burgers—the kind of food Terry never cooked—and I listened to them talk about people I didn't know.

At one point, one of the women said, "Whatever happened to Samantha?" and I found that I wasn't overcome with jealousy or sorrow. I listened closely. I wanted to know.

Billy said, "We don't really know. She probably went back to Ukiah."

"She had a friend from high school there," Liz said. "A girl she could stay with. That's our best guess."

The conversation moved on and we finished our meals. Darkness had fallen by the time we'd said our goodbyes and started the drive back. I was in the middle seat again. I kept thinking of Samantha. I was ready to know instead of wonder.

"You all liked her a lot, right? Samantha?" I asked.

Billy shrugged. "She was okay. I mean, I don't know. I don't know what to say about her, really."

"She was cool," Liz said. "She wasn't *you*, but she was fine."

I felt their shoulders touching mine, felt myself smile in the dark.

Once we got back to the farm, we unloaded all our trades into the refrigerator and pantry and handed the money to Julia.

"Everyone loved the zinnias today," Liz said.

"And the dahlias," I said.

Julia beamed. "Good, good," she said. "And did you have fun?"

"I love it there," I said. "I've never been to a town like that."

We told her where we went to dinner and what we all ordered, who we saw there and the gossip we heard.

"A million people said to tell you hello," Billy said.

"As usual," Liz added.

"Hello to a million people." Julia laughed. "Well, you'll rest well tonight."

We headed across the field, back to our cabins. My shoulders were sore from carrying the crates and buckets, but I didn't want to be alone. I steeled myself for our goodbye—for the two of them to walk into one cabin, shut the door, and leave me outside—but when we reached Liz's door, she said, "Who wants to share a bottle of wine?"

We went into our cabins for thicker sweaters and socks and one glass each before meeting back outside Liz's cabin, where we sat together in a row, facing the field. The ghosts were out, but they didn't seem to mind us. Seeing so many of them together like that, I realized that most of them were very small. A few of them were taller, a couple were almost grown-up. But most of them were children. A few of the older ones were huddled in a group, and another broke away from them. *Oh*, I realized as she began to dance—it was her. I looked away.

"Here," Liz said, filling my glass.

"Terry and Julia don't care?" I asked.

"It's a *glass* of wine. But no, I don't think so. They let us have some on holidays."

I took a sip. I'd only tried wine a couple times before and had never cared much about it, but this tasted good. Maybe it was just the moment, sitting there with them in the cool night air. Maybe I would have liked anything, when it was Billy and Liz and me in the moonlight.

The ghosts played on the grass. The dancing ghost was spinning and spinning. I looked away and saw Billy, watching me.

"She's showing off for you, you know," Billy said.

"Who?" I asked.

"Your ghost."

"She hurts my eyes."

"You'll get used to it."

"I like to watch them," Liz said, gazing onto the field. "They always look so happy."

It was true. A group of ghost children played together, some kind of game I didn't know. One of them seemed to count and the others scattered, running in all directions. They were too far away; I couldn't see their faces. But I could tell by the way they moved in hops and skips that they were enjoying themselves.

Liz said, "Yours is such a beautiful dancer. I like watching her the best."

"I don't know why you all call her mine."

She looked at me. "You don't?"

"No."

She turned back to the dancing ghost.

"Okay," she said.

Billy stood up and stretched. I thought he was going to say good night, but instead he strode into the field, right to the center of the children's game. The little ones gathered around him, just as Darius and James and Blanca and Mackenzie did every day. I could tell he was explaining something to them and they were listening, and then together they began to play a new game. The dancing ghost didn't pay attention. She spun and leapt. A small group of ghosts who had been sitting together looked over but then stood and walked away. Billy fell onto the grass with a giant *whoop* that carried across the distance and the ghost children piled on top of him. We could hear his laughter.

"I didn't even know we could interact with them like that," I said.

"Last Christmas the preschoolers got to stay up late and they played with them. It was so cute to watch. I don't know if *cute*'s the word. Cute-sad. You know. Terry keeps his distance, out of respect, I think. And Julia doesn't like to look at them." She sipped, swallowed. "Some people don't see them at all."

"Really?"

"Yeah. You'll see at Thanksgiving. There are always a few people who have no clue what we're talking about."

"They must think we're crazy," I said.

"Mila," she said. "Look at them. Clear as anything. Nobody's crazy here. We just see different things."

Billy was pretending to be an airplane, tearing across the field with two little ghosts on his back. When the game ended, he crossed the field and came back to us, smelling like grass and sweat. He sat, and Liz handed him the bottle, and the three of us stayed out for another hour together in our layers of sweaters and socks, watching the ghosts.

———————

The next morning, when I gave Lee the paints, his eyes grew wide and happy. "Yippee!" he said, and hugged the tin to his heart.

"I hope you'll show me what you paint," I told him.

"I will," he said.

And all through that day's lesson, I caught him in moments of quiet smiles, saw him touch the smooth handle of the brush with the tip of a finger, or feel the rough tooth of the paper. And I felt a gladness in my own heart that I'd given the gift to him, that I'd found this way to make him happy.

I am good, I thought. *I am good.*

Later, when I went to the house to help with dinner, Lee called me into the living room.

"Close your eyes and hold out your hands," he said. I felt a paper placed into my palms. "Now open!"

He covered his own face with a pillow and hummed with anticipation as I looked at what he had given me.

A watercolor painting of the two of us, standing in the green field under a blue sky and a happy sun, holding hands. Our names were written in pencil below our figures. *Mila. Lee.*

"Oh, buddy," I said. "This looks just like us!"

"It *does*?"

"It does! I love it. Thank you."

"Oh, and I found this upstairs. I think it will fit." He showed me a wood frame without anything in it, just the glass over a cardboard back.

"How perfect," I said. "You just found it?"

"There's a lot of stuff in that closet."

I nodded, remembering that Julia had told me that same thing. The paint was dry, so I took the back off the frame and set the paper in. I pushed down the metal tabs and turned it around. There we were, Lee and me. "I can't wait to hang this in my cabin," I told him, and he gave me another one of the smiles I so loved.

I hoped Lee was doing better. That he was less haunted and afraid, and it had not only been celebrations and watercolors that had cheered him. But a few days later, his smiles were gone again. He was distracted during lessons, no matter how hard I tried to engage him.

"Soon, we'll have two new friends," I told him. "It will be so nice for you to be around other kids your own age."

"Yeah," he said, but he stared out the window, expressionless, until it was time for math. He opened his textbook. I let him work on his own while I reviewed our art textbooks for what we'd study next. Though I was grateful for my time with Lee, I looked forward to having three students instead of only one. Across the schoolhouse, Liz led Emma and Jackson and Hunter in a discussion of some kind. And farther still, the little ones sprawled on the floor listening to Billy read. When I glanced at Lee's paper to see how he was doing, I saw more blacked-out squares than ever before.

"I just can't get it right," he said. "I'm so *stupid*."

"Let's go outside," I told him. "Why don't we race?"

He shut the textbook, rested his head atop its cover. "I'm too tired for racing," he said.

"Has it been . . . hard for you here, Lee?" I asked him later on in the living room. We were on the sofa, the fire crackling in the hearth. "Have you been lonely?"

"Not lonely," he said. "Just scared."

"Scared about what?"

"My ghost."

"Oh," I said. "I see. Is he still making mean faces?"

Lee nodded.

"I've been thinking," I said. "You know how, that day when we were drawing, we talked about how it's good to look at what scares us? That it makes the fear go away?"

"Yeah."

"Maybe," I said, taking in a breath. "Maybe the fear doesn't ever actually *go away*. Maybe we have to keep on working. We thought it would be simple, but it isn't. We thought we could be finished, but maybe . . . maybe we'll never be entirely finished."

His face crumpled in sadness. "But I want it to be over."

"I know, Lee," I said. I put my arm around him. "I want that, too. But do you think we could ever—do you think it might be possible—to be happy anyway?"

"I can try," he said.

"I'll try too," I told him. People were in the kitchen, in the upstairs room. I wanted to tell Lee more but I didn't want anyone else to hear me. I scooted closer to him and whispered, "I'm scared too. I'm scared all the time. I keep having these memories that turn real. There was a shell in a memory—a shell used to trick me—I stepped on it—I found real blood on my foot. Blood from just the memory of it. And I don't like the ghosts, especially the one who dances. She hurts my eyes."

At first, he didn't respond, but then he looked at me. He blinked back tears. "Sometimes I feel like I'm going to split in half," he said. "It hurts that much."

"Oh no," I said. "Oh, Lee. Come here."

He scooted closer, rested his head on my shoulder. I put my arm around him and we sat on the living room sofa, both of us quiet for a long time. We belonged together—our bare wrists, our hauntings. He was my family more than any of the others. I would do my best to help him, with whatever limited understanding I had.

"Mila, you ready?" Liz called from the kitchen. We were on dinner prep tonight.

"Go ahead," Lee said, sitting up.

I put my hand on his cheek. "Are you sure?" I asked.

He nodded but I still saw sadness in his eyes. I hadn't done enough, but I couldn't think of anything else to try.

The next Sunday's market was teeming with people trying to get the last of the season's tomatoes, sitting on the benches and curbs in the sunshine, knowing cooler weather would soon sweep in. We'd almost sold out of everything, only had a little left to trade. Liz bought a stack of novels from the bookstore with her day's earnings. I saved mine. I didn't know what I was saving up for, but it felt safer to keep it.

We spent the late afternoon on the beach, resting our bodies after all the time on our feet, and back at the farm we stayed up late again, watching the ghosts on the green again, drinking tea this time as the night grew late.

"Tell me about your lives before," I asked them. It took courage, but I wanted to know so badly, knew I had to ask.

"My moms were total nomads," Billy said. "We traveled all over the country in an Airstream. I got homeschooled, but mostly we just didn't care about school. We cared about canyons and lakes and birds and the sun. But they were both estranged from their families, so when they died, I went straight into the system."

I wanted to know how they died, but he would have told me if he'd wanted me to know. Instead I asked, "How old were you?"

"Twelve," he said.

"I'm sorry," I told him.

He tipped his face up to the moonlight. Closed his eyes. Opened them. "Thank you," he said.

I looked at Liz. She took a sip of her tea.

"I was raised by wolves." She turned to me and smiled.

"Funny," I said, smiling back. "So was I."

When I finally returned to my cabin, the night was deep and black and most of the ghosts had vanished. I built a fire and undressed. I pulled my nightgown over my head.

It was the dead of night. My mother was working at the diner. Blake was asleep. I climbed down the steep slope of Blake's property and onto the street. Several blocks away was a convenience store that still had a pay phone. I carried coins in my fist. It had taken me a week to scavenge enough change for a call—a nickel one day, a dime the next—and every night as I burrowed into my sleeping bag, I played it out in my mind: I would dial my grandparents' number. *I need you*, I would say. Minutes later, their white car would pull up in front of the store and they'd hold me, they'd rescue me, they'd never let me go.

I reached the pay phone, stood in the neon light of store. Each coin in my fingertips was a wish. I pushed them, one after the next, into the slot. The phone rang. *It's okay—they're just sleeping.* Rang and rang. *Soon Grammy will sit up in bed.* Rang and rang. *Or I'll leave a message and tell them where to find me.* Rang and rang and rang and rang, until a man waiting tapped me on the shoulder. When he was finished with his call, I tried again. I tried five more times before giving up.

Sometimes, not often, my mother and I were alone together.

When will we see them? I wanted to ask her. It felt impossible that they would stay away from us for so long on purpose, impossible that my mother would not take me back to them. Why were we living in a house that was not a house? How had we come to be this way?

When we were alone, I would look for an opening. For something in her face. For her to take me in her arms. *Mama*, I would say to her. *What's happened to us?*

But we'd barely begin to talk when my mother would feel her ear, notice another earring missing. "Help me find it," she'd say. We'd look through the dirt and the brush and the poppies, across the concrete foundation of the house, through the eucalyptus leaves and their strips of dead bark. We'd search for tiny, precious things and we would never find them.

Once, I was no larger than a fleck of dust but she loved me.

I turned away from her as she touched her swollen earlobe. As she cursed and cried at her own carelessness. As she waited for Blake to come home so she could confess.

He always forgave her. She'd press herself against him, her face full of gratitude and regret. They'd close the curtains to his room as though that kept the sound out. A couple days later, he'd give her another pair to make up for the loss.

Sometimes I was permitted to leave the property for the library or the convenience store. I read books on the brain. I read books on the reproductive system, searching for the things Blake told us. I was not surprised to find that none of it was true. At the library's clean tables, I tried to remember how to play the piano. I placed my fingers on the tabletop and pressed imaginary keys. Whenever I saw coins on the sidewalk I picked them up, pushed them into the slot of the convenience store's pay phone. I called my grandparents but no one answered. It just rang and rang. I wanted to call Hayley but I hadn't ever memorized her number. Day after day, I climbed high up Blake's hill. He had built a platform there, on the exposed roots of an ancient, upturned tree. I would wait with the opera glasses, and if I was lucky I'd find my ghost. Such a sad old woman. Such hollow eyes. But it comforted me to see her.

Lorna, I would whisper. *Hello*, I would say.

Some days, she held strange things in her hands. Some days, she had nothing. I thanked her for letting me see her. I said, *If there is anything you need, just tell me.* I wanted to ask for her help, too. To get me away from there. To deliver a message to my grandparents. I imagined her showing up at their front door, a nightgowned ghost framed by the potted ferns, holding a letter from me in her hand. They would read it and rush to my rescue.

Or, if not that much, I wanted my mother to see her so I wouldn't be so alone.

Maybe, if she appeared to my mother, my mother would become herself again.

But she was dreaming and waking without me. No more slipping into our shared room in the early mornings. No more staying up after dark. No more secret smiles that warmed me until I was full of feeling and light.

Instead she was with Blake, always. He would bring her more gifts and she would, again, inexplicably, lose them. He made a big production out of each pair of earrings, describing how he persuaded the shop owner to sell him her most valuable things and how she'd regretted parting with them. "Too late now," he'd say, pushing a new pair in. My mother always smiled, but we didn't have a clean bathroom counter to store things. Didn't have rubbing alcohol or cotton balls, and her left earlobe was red and tender, and each time he put them in I wondered if he could see how it hurt her.

Until, one day, during a time when my mother had been more quiet than usual, distracted and sad, he told us there were going to be changes to the house. "A master suite, for my bride," he said. "It's going to be out of a magazine, Miriam. You will hardly believe it."

"Will it have a ceiling?" I asked.

He laughed. "Of course. And a floor—*marble*. And an en suite bathroom with a spa tub and gold fixtures."

"Will the whole house have a roof now?" I asked, thinking of the nights I spent shivering.

"Patience, Mila," he told me. "Good things take time."

I gasped, surfacing. I was on my hands and knees, panting in front of the woodstove—*too hot, too close.* I crawled to the door, desperate for air, and managed to stand long enough to open it and stagger out.

I had what I wanted now. The market with Billy and Liz. Lee's trust, Terry's and Julia's friendship. The little ones asked me for help when they needed it, showed me their creations, told me their funny ideas. Even Jackson and Emma and Hunter seemed to like me. I had a home there. I didn't need to go back—not ever, not even in my mind. I could live among the ghosts. I could watch them and respect them and not need to understand.

I was leaning against my cabin wall, alone in the dark. I would find my way back to myself. Soon, my heart would calm, beat by beat. It had to.

I took in a breath. Smelled metal. I looked around for the rusted wheelbarrow or a stray bucket, but all I saw was the path and some grass and the gravel. Slowly, I lifted my hands to my nose.

The scent of coins on my skin, unmistakable.

A cry escaped me.

How I'd clenched them in my fist.

How desperately I had hoped.

Coin in the slot, over and over.

"Mila?" It was Liz, walking toward me in the dark. "Are you okay?"

"Something is wrong with me." I was shaking so violently my teeth chattered. No way to hide it. "I don't know what it is."

"You're *scared,*" Liz said. "That's all. Come with me."

I followed her to her cabin, which was just like my own. Billy was there, too, blowing out a match, closing the door of the wood-burning stove.

"Sit here," Liz said, pulling her chair in front of the fire. She draped her quilt over my shoulders.

"You can talk to us," Billy said, sitting at my feet.

"We're here for you," Liz said, settling beside him.

"I won't make any sense," I said. "I'm having these memories. They swallow me up. And something is *after* me."

"Why do you think that?" Liz asked.

I shook my head. I didn't know how to explain without telling them everything, and they'd be horrified if I told them the truth. I could have left the skeleton house. I could have left Blake and my mother. I could have found myself help, and made myself a different life—one still of heartache, yes, but not of hauntings.

I had a choice, and I made the wrong one.

They could not know. I would not tell them.

But how could I carry it with me any longer?

I had to get this sick thing outside of me. Had to speak it, but could not tell them. "When I was young," I said, "I did a horrible thing. And I'm afraid that it's followed me here."

I thought it might ruin everything, just speaking those words. Letting them know that I was not perfect. I was not good. They'd realize they were mistaken to have ever thought I was someone to befriend.

But Liz nodded and whispered, "Okay."

Silence filled the cabin.

Then Billy said, "I had these *pains* when I got here. Sometimes in my chest, sometimes in my leg. They would shoot up both arms, just all of a sudden."

Liz listened while he spoke. When he was finished, she said, "I saw horrible things. *Nightmare* things. When I thought everything was fine, there they would be."

"Really?" I asked them.

"Yes, really," they said.

"It's hard," Liz said. "It hurts. *All* of it does. We understand."

My hands stopped trembling. I shrugged the quilt off my shoulders.

Billy, now warm, slid off his jacket, and I found that he possessed a new kind of beauty with his tired eyes, the curve of his shoulders through his cotton shirt. And Liz, too, with the glow of warm light on her skin, the openness in her face as she watched me. There we were in the first cabin, across the field from everyone else, all by ourselves.

I'd felt so awkward around them, and unfamiliar, and aware of the things I didn't know. But now a different feeling emerged. One of how they were holding me, even as they sat a distance away. How they were anchoring me to the earth.

"Stay with us," Liz said. "Stay tonight. Sleep here."

I had felt so alone, but here were Liz and Billy. Here they were, offering me this.

"If you're sure," I told them.

"We're sure. And I can sleep on the floor if that would be better," Billy said.

But I wanted warmth. I wanted comfort. So we slept in Liz's bed, the three of together, as the night wore on. Such a small space for three fully grown people, with no room for uncertainty. No room for ghosts.

———

After that, most nights we all slept together, in one bed or another. It didn't matter whose. Our cabins were their own little country, the field an ocean separating us from the others. Sometimes, when it was windy and the goats had neglected it, the long grasses even rippled like waves.

Sometimes Billy and Liz slipped out in the cold mornings, the two of them together, for the shower. They spent a long time away, and I pretended not to mind, tried not to think of their naked bodies, the heat they generated without me. My jealousy was a small thing to suffer, though, compared with all they gave me. They made it so easy to pretend nothing had ever appeared on my doorstep, that memories had never swallowed me whole, that I had never feared Blake's ghost, lurking among the others.

But every few nights I woke while the two of them were fast asleep. I'd wrap myself in Liz's robe or Billy's jacket, tiptoe out of the cabin and into the night. I'd sit outside the door, listening to the wind and ocean, the moon shining above me. I was waiting for something—offering myself up to whatever was out there—but it didn't come. And after a time, I'd grow too cold, too tired, and I'd give up and go back in. Into the warm room, into the warm bed, pressed against the bodies of my friends.

Weekdays we spent as we always did, teaching in the schoolhouse, helping out with dinner. Saturdays we hiked together, up through the headlands, adorned with wildflowers and manzanita. Billy taught me the names of all the plants and Liz found ways to surprise us. Sketchbooks and colored pencils one day. A picnic the next.

What are they doing with me? I caught myself wondering. I didn't know how I could possibly be special enough for them. So I posed on the rocks and let them draw me by the ocean. Once, I spent all the money I'd saved and made us reservations at a fancy restaurant, where the hostess took our jackets at the door and our waiter folded the napkin of whoever went to use the restroom. When it was time for dessert, two men torched the sugar tops of our crème brûlées at the table. We cracked them open with our spoons.

You're incredible, they said to me. I tried to believe them.

And sometimes we watched the ghosts, and Billy asked me to look closely, but it hurt my eyes if I did it for longer than a few moments at a time. And sometimes I caught Billy and Liz watching *me*, expressions on their faces that I couldn't understand. I told myself it was nothing. Tried to believe that, too.

They wanted to teach me to surf, but I couldn't take the shock of the water. I spent most of the time on the sand, watching them in their wet suits, amazed by my luck. Sundays, we woke so early our bodies wondered why we weren't sleeping. In darkness, Terry's lanterns slung over our arms, we carried the buckets of blossoms Julia had prepared for us, loaded the squashes and bunches of kale in their crates, latched the back of the pickup truck, and headed to Mendocino. Up and down that winding highway, I sat in between them, always. When Billy drove, Liz rested her head on my shoulder.

I'd never been so happy.

APART FROM OUR WEEKDAY LESSONS in the schoolhouse, I was spending less time with Lee. I'd suggest a hike or an afternoon with our watercolors, but more often than not he'd say no.

He was receding into himself, never eager anymore, rarely speaking.

One Saturday I went to find him in the house, hoping we'd put a puzzle together or play a board game. Jackson and Emma lounged outside, enjoying a rare sunny hour. Julia and Terry were in the kitchen, engrossed in intimate conversation. Hunter supervised the little ones as they played.

"Have you seen Lee?" I asked him.

"Not for a while," Hunter said.

I walked up the stairs, but Lee's door was ajar and I saw he wasn't in his room. On my way back down, little James said, "I see Lee!"

"You see him?" I asked.

"I tink he pay-ing hide-and-seek!"

"Where?" I said. "Will you show me?"

James wrapped his hand around one of my fingers and led me to a small door under the staircase. I had never noticed it before.

"He *inside*," James said, pointing.

"In here?" I asked, a chill running through me.

James nodded and scurried away.

Could it be true? The door was half-sized, like the entry to a crawl space. I put my ear close to the wood and heard a movement. Slowly, I turned the knob, eased it open.

The toe of a shoe, the hem of a pant leg.

"Lee," I said. "*Buddy*. What are you doing in here?"

"Hiding," Lee said. He had his arms around his knees, was rocking forward and back.

I bent to fit under the door frame and stepped, still crouching, inside.

"Shut the door," he said, so I did. Light came from a bare bulb overhead. I sat cross-legged next to him. "What are you hiding *from*?" I asked.

"My ghost. I think." His eyes filled with tears.

"*Oh, Lee*," I said.

"I don't know what's happening."

"Whatever it is," I said, "I'll protect you."

"I don't think you can. He's getting closer."

"What do you mean?"

"He gets *closer* and *closer*."

"But he isn't here now, is he?"

"I don't know," Lee said. "The light is on."

"Should we turn it off and check?"

He startled at the suggestion. "*No!*" he said.

"Okay," I assured him. "We don't have to. I would never *make* you do anything, Lee. Nothing that you didn't want to do. But I don't think he's here. I really don't. It's only you and me."

He nodded, and my heart ached for him. His little furrowed brow. His callused hands and his crooked finger. I touched his earlobe, small and perfect. "I'll always protect you," I said. "For as long as we are here together."

He nodded. "Okay, Mila."

I put my arm around him and felt his body lean into mine. He smelled like grass, like earth, like early mornings.

"I'll never leave you," I said to him. I closed my eyes. I felt his body relaxing, heard the slowing of his breath. "You'll have to grow up and leave me first."

Time passed and my legs started aching. I endured the discomfort as long as I could, but when I tried to shift positions without bothering him, he sat up. "We can go back out now," he said. "I feel better."

So I opened the closet door, and he pulled the chain to turn off the light. I stepped out and he followed. Until now, I'd felt that I could take care of him myself, but as I watched him climb the stairs on his own, I knew that I couldn't. He had always been anxious and easily startled, but to hide in a closet under the stairs? To huddle in a ball and rock himself? To talk so desperately about his ghost? All of that was new.

Terry was in the kitchen tending to his bread.

"Do you have a minute?" I asked him.

"Always," he said.

So I told him what had happened as he kneaded. I had expected some alarm, but, though he listened closely and appeared concerned, he didn't seem surprised. "Thank you for telling me, Mila," he said when I had finished. "That was the right thing to do. He's upstairs now?"

"Yes."

He crossed to the sink. "I want you to know . . . ," he said as the water ran, as he picked the soap off its dish and rubbed it between his palms. "You are a true friend to Lee." I let his words linger as he dried his hands on a cloth.

He paused before he left the kitchen to place a hand on my shoulder.

"A true friend to *all* of us," he said.

Later, in Billy's cabin, Liz strummed a ukulele while Billy read silently from a book of poems. I lay in the center of the bed, staring at the darkness through the skylight, thinking of Lee. Finally I sat up. Billy lowered his book. Liz let the instrument lie in her lap.

"What is it?" she asked.

So I told her about how James had led me to Lee. About finding him, so frightened, in the closet.

"Terry told us," Billy said.

"Oh," I said. "Okay." I thought it strange that they would not have mentioned it to me. Would not have checked in to see how I was, or asked for more details to fill in the story. But, as though reading my mind, Liz said, "We wanted to give you time. It must have been upsetting, seeing him like that."

"It was," I said, lowering back onto the bed. I saw him rocking back and forth, remembered my promise to always protect him, renewed it for myself right then. Soon the bed dipped with weight on both sides of me. Liz was there, propped on her elbow, behind me. "You did the right thing," she said. "You did exactly what you needed to do, and now Terry is taking care of him."

Billy smiled at me, his face next to mine on the pillow. "She's right," he said. "Everything's going to turn out okay."

With the two of them beside me, their low voices comforting me, I allowed myself to close my eyes. Soon, I drifted to sleep. No nightmares, no visions of men come to haunt me or scared little boys rocking forward and back. No sickness over the things I had or had not done. Only assurances that I was good, that I did what I should have, that Lee was all right now—all those sweet words whispered into my ears.

And then I woke up alone.

The bed was cold. I reached for the blankets and they gave too easily, no bodies tangled up in them. I sat and saw the emptiness.

In those first bleary, disoriented moments, I thought maybe it all had been a dream. That I had not, in fact, been so lucky. That I had been alone in my own bed all those nights, imagining they were with me. We'd never dressed up for dinner, I'd never held still and let them draw me, had not learned the names of the wildflowers after all.

But my vision sharpened and I saw more of the cabin. Billy's, not mine. So, where *were* they?

I rose from bed and made my way to the window. I could make out figures on the field—*human* figures, not glowing. A full moon hung above them, lighting the sky enough for me to see. Liz and Terry, with Lee between them. All three stood still, as though they were waiting for something. I wanted to go to them, but I was aware of a strangeness, an intensity, and I stayed at the window, watching.

Soon, something in the distance caught my eye, and as it came closer I saw that it was Billy and a ghost child. Maybe the one who'd been making faces at Lee through the window, I thought, though they were too far away to know. Billy held the ghost's hand as they made their way to the others. When the five of them were together, the adults sat on the grass and Lee and the ghost child did the same. I saw that they were talking. Liz slipped her arm around Lee's waist and I felt my stomach tighten. *Lee was mine.* Terry rested his broad palm on Lee's head, let it slip to his shoulder, where it rested for a few moments. I saw Lee nod. And then the ghost child scooted onto Lee's lap. Lee held him the way he would have held a little brother, the way he held the little ones sometimes, for a book or a song.

I was entranced by it, confused by it. I was fixed to the window, hidden in the dark. And then Lee screamed.

Out of the cabin I flew, across the path to the field in my thin nightclothes and my bare feet.

"Lee!" I called, and Liz turned to me in alarm. I could hear Lee, crying now, but Billy had him in his arms and I couldn't see Lee's face, couldn't see what had hurt him. The ghost was nowhere in sight—I must have scared him off—and I knew Lee would have wanted me with him, to comfort him. It was Lee and me, more than anyone else. *I* was who he trusted. *I* was who he loved. But something about all of them together made me slow my pace. I stopped short, on the periphery.

"What happened?" I asked. "Does he need help?"

Terry turned as though he were surprised to see me, as though he hadn't heard my yell. His face was all urgency and worry and impatience. No gentleness in it. He held a palm out to stop me from getting any closer. "We've got this," he said. "We don't need you right now."

I froze in shame. Took a step back.

Billy and Liz and Terry. Suddenly strangers. *Who were these people who pretended to love me?*

"I need to know that Lee is okay," I said, my voice loud and trembling.

"He's fine," Terry said. "He'll be fine. Go back in now. I told you—we've got this."

So away I went, not back to Billy's cabin, but back to my own, and closed the door against all of them. Outside in the dark, Lee was still crying. I pressed my pillow over my ears. My bed was cold as winter.

At breakfast the next morning, I didn't look at any of them. I served myself toast and a boiled egg and kale and sat at the far end of the table, away from Billy and Liz.

"Hey," Billy said. "Good morning."

I rose to pour myself a cup of coffee.

The little ones had egg all over their hands, so I dampened a cloth and wiped their tiny fingers. Emma and Jackson and Hunter got up and cleared their dishes.

"I'll be in the schoolhouse in a few minutes," Liz told them. "You can get started with the chapter."

And then the high schoolers were gone, and the little ones were lost in their own worlds. I felt the intensity of Terry and Liz and Billy staring at me. Looked up and found it to be true.

"Where's Lee?" I asked.

"He'll be staying in bed today," Terry told me. "He's tired and needs to rest. Julia's up there now to check on him."

I nodded. Chewed and swallowed. Found I wasn't hungry.

I heard Julia's footsteps coming down the stairs.

"Mila," she said. "I need to get ready for the twins to arrive. They'll be here soon. Would you be willing to help me? After we're done, you can have the rest of the day for lesson planning in the schoolhouse."

I cleared my dishes.

The rest of them still sat at the table. I followed Julia out of the kitchen.

I'd been upstairs only a few times over the months I'd lived on the farm—last night when I'd gone searching for Lee, once to help wash the little ones' hair, once to carry a chair from the basement up to Lee's room. He'd wanted a place of his own to read. I passed his room now, paused to listen. Only silence. I touched the door as though it could tell me something, and then followed Julia down the hall. There were three bedrooms on the second story: Lee's; the little ones'; and one that would soon belong to the twins. The teenagers lived in the two attic rooms, and Terry and Julia's bedroom was downstairs. The house seemed to go on forever.

Julia stepped through the door at the end of the hall.

A slanted ceiling. Two wicker beds, with a circular rag rug between them. She set the sheets down, opened the window to let in the breeze. We made one of the beds and then the other. We wiped dust from the dresser and fluffed the pillows.

She swept the floor and I swept the cobwebs out of the corners, and then—already—we heard a car on the drive. I looked over the room, wondered how I'd feel to find out it was mine. It was sweet and girlish, with hand-stitched quilts. Worn, not precious. I would have liked it, had I moved here when I was young.

I watched Julia straighten a picture frame, lay out a lace over the top of the dresser.

What do you know about Lee? I wanted to ask her. *What happened to him last night?*

But I couldn't get the words out. The car doors were slamming shut. I heard the crunch of gravel, the front door open.

"Shall we greet your new students?" she asked, as though nothing were wrong. As though Lee weren't closed up in his room, suffering from something terrible.

"I don't know," I said.

She cocked her head, perplexed, and I couldn't tell if she was feigning her confusion.

"Lee . . . ," I started, but didn't finish. I wanted to curl up in one of the beds we'd just made. Wanted to sleep in this child's room and wake up young and unafraid.

But Julia ushered me to the door and out. "He'll be all right," she said in the hallway. "He just needs to rest. And *we* need to head downstairs. Our girls are waiting."

Diamond and Ruby were seated in the kitchen, their eyes wide, taking everything in. They were fair and chubby, with light brown wavy hair. Ruby wore a T-shirt with a unicorn on it, Diamond a pink-and-yellow-striped sweater.

I knew that one day they'd awaken to a breakfast tray to celebrate their birthdays. They'd outgrow their old clothes and start blending in with everyone else, in simple shirts and wool sweaters, soft corduroys and jeans. They'd play and laugh. But, for now, they were straddling two lives. I remembered what it was like, not even so long ago, first stepping foot into this one. Did they feel the same wonder I did? The same dizziness, the same tremor of something uncertain beneath?

Terry set mugs of hot chocolate in front them. Ruby looked at Diamond and waited. Diamond took a sip, so Ruby did, too.

Julia sat at the table and had me slide in next to her.

"Girls," she said. "We're so happy to have you here, after all these months of waiting. This is Mila, she'll be your teacher. And you have a classmate, Lee, who isn't feeling well today, but will be up and eager to meet you tomorrow."

The girls nodded.

I said, "Tell me what you like to do. What's your favorite subject in school?"

"Math," said Ruby.

"Art," said Diamond.

"All right," I said. "Good. We can do both of those things. I even know ways we can do them at the same time."

Julia squeezed my knee under the table.

Sometimes, I was so close to being one of them. So convincing, I almost convinced myself.

I sat with Ruby and Diamond at dinnertime and afterward I read them a book by the fire. When Julia was ready to take them upstairs, I was part relieved, part distressed to see Billy and Liz were gone already.

But they were waiting for me outside of my cabin. I walked in and they followed. We stood inside together, the three of us, silent. Billy by the stove, Liz leaning against the desk, me in the center of the room. I felt the prick of tears, tried to fight them.

"Mila," Liz said. "We wanted you to know . . . last night wasn't what it looked like. It wasn't . . . *bad*."

"Then what *was* it?"

"We want to make sure you know we're here for you," Billy said. "What you're going through—we don't want you to be alone."

"But I wasn't alone," I said. "I was with you. And then you snuck away and you did something to Lee and I don't even know who you are."

"*No,*" Liz said. "We didn't do anything to him. You don't understand."

"Then tell me! I cook and I clean. I wake up at five a.m. with you and work the stand and I *like* it. I live surrounded by ghosts. I sleep in your bed. I love Lee and I'm as good to him as I know how to be. What else do I need to do?"

"*Mila.*" Liz pulled me close. She pressed her lips against my cheek and my heart gave me away. My eyes fluttered shut. To be touched like this, to be kissed by her. Billy stepped behind me, wrapped his arms around me.

I heard him murmur into my hair, "It's okay, Mila."

"You're one of us," Liz said.

But at her words, my body went stiff. I opened my eyes to my cabin, and I didn't know why I was standing there, why these bodies were pressed against me. On my wall was the watercolor of Lee and me, the only thing I owned that meant anything.

"I need to be alone," I told them. And they let me go.

Hours later, alone in my cabin, all I could think of was Lee. The way he'd cradled the little ghost. His scream and his cries. I needed to see him. And I felt that he couldn't possibly be sleeping. Whatever happened must have unsettled him enough that he'd be, at the very least, fitful and in and out of dreams. I went to my window and looked across the field to the house. A faint light glowed from his upstairs bedroom.

It was almost midnight. I put on my coat, slipped on my shoes, turned on the lantern. I crossed the field and let myself into the kitchen. As quietly as I could, I took a carton of milk from the refrigerator and a small pot off the rack. I turned the burner on low and poured in enough milk for one small mug. As I opened the spice drawer for cinnamon and clove, I heard a light switch on in the living room, but I didn't stop what I was doing.

I wouldn't let them hide him away. Not any longer.

In the pantry, I found the honey Liz had traded for at the market a few weeks ago. It was thick and sweet and I took a heaping spoonful of it and stirred it into the warmed milk. I added one clove and a sprinkle of cinnamon and poured in a drop of vanilla.

The milk was warm enough now. As I turned the burner off, I heard music come from the piano. Familiar notes.

It was the opening refrain of "Someone to Watch Over Me."

I stood still at the stove as the song continued, unsure what to make of it. Terry or Julia, I guessed. Was it some sort of comment on my presence there, so late at night? Was it a *joke*?

I filled the mug with the milk, set the pan in the sink, and made my way to the doorway.

No one was at the piano.

But the melody filled the room, in spite of the emptiness.

And then I saw the piano keys, moving on their own.

I shut off the light and in darkness there she was, the

dancing ghost, seated at the piano, but I could only stand to see her for a fraction of a moment—she hurt my eyes, she made me dizzy—so I snapped the light back on and she disappeared. No more music. Just me, alone, in the dimly lit room.

Until Terry emerged from his bedroom and stood in the darkened doorway.

"I heard you playing."

"It wasn't me," I told him.

He didn't say anything more, just looked at me. I couldn't tell if there was something else he wanted to say. The room was silent, and all I wanted was to see Lee. I would forget all the rest of it. It was stupid and small. As if a little piano playing would scare me away. As if a man, standing quietly in pajamas, would be enough to stop me.

"Lee's awake. I'm bringing him some warm milk." I started up the stairs and didn't look back.

I tapped on Lee's door, quietly so as to not wake the others. "Lee," I said. "It's me. I'm coming in."

I turned the knob and entered. He was sitting up in bed. He looked glad to see me.

"Hey, buddy," I said to him.

"I couldn't sleep," he told me.

"I know. I saw the light on in your window."

"You did? From all the way in your cabin?"

I nodded. "I brought you some warm milk. It used to help me fall asleep. Want to try it?"

He nodded and I sat next to him on the edge of the bed. He took the mug in both hands. "Yum," he said after the first sip.

He looked even skinnier than usual in his short-sleeved nightshirt and shorts. Why didn't Julia have him in long sleeves and pants? *I* was the one who knew what Lee needed. I crossed to his chest of drawers and found a light sweatshirt.

"Are you wearing socks?"

He shook his head, so I found him a pair of socks, too.

When he'd finished the last of the milk, I helped him put on the sweatshirt and watched as he pulled the socks over his feet. I straightened the tip of one of the socks so that the hem lined up with his toes.

"Think you can sleep now?" I asked.

"I think so." He lay down and I smoothed his hair away from his face. With his eyes closed, he looked even younger than his nine years. His little curved nose. His long eyelashes, his sweet mouth. "Stay with me until I fall asleep?" he asked.

"Of course," I said. I switched off his light and took his hand in mine so he'd know I was there. "Are you okay, buddy?" I said, my eyes adjusting to the dark.

"Yeah," he said. "It really hurt, but I'm okay now."

I held his hand as his breathing steadied and slowed, until his fingers relaxed from mine. "*What* really hurt, Lee?" I finally asked, but he was deep in sleep by then.

I stayed for a few more minutes. If he woke again, I didn't want him to find me gone. I sat, looking at his young face, and then I allowed myself to scan past his fingers, past his palm, to where a gold chain circled his wrist.

Back outside, the cold wind hit me. The moon was obscured by clouds and the ghosts were everywhere, darting through the dark. More of them than I had ever seen. I hunched my shoulders and kept my head down as I took the long way around the field, not wanting to walk among them. But even though I tried not to look, I saw the dancing girl break away from a group of other ghosts and move nearer to me, to the edge of the grass. I felt her gaze as I walked, and it filled me with a fury that tilted my vision and made me tremble.

I wanted her to go back to the others.

I needed her to stop staring.

But she stood still and watched as I walked and I wanted to disappear. I understood why Samantha would have left suddenly, without saying goodbye to any of them.

I felt the ghost's eyes on me, unrelenting.

"Leave me the fuck alone!" I screamed, my voice raw and monstrous. I barely recognized it as my own.

She disappeared. A final blow—that she could do so easily what I couldn't do myself. But at least she was gone and I could make the rest of the walk with no one watching me.

a day & a night

I HAD THREE PUPILS NOW, in my corner of the schoolhouse.

"Lee, why don't you show the girls where the supplies are kept?" I said, and Lee—clear-eyed and eager, any trace of fear or sorrow gone—sprang from his chair.

"Come with me," he told Ruby and Diamond, and led them to the supply cabinet. I listened for a little while as he told them where the pencils and sharpeners were kept, where the paper was stacked and what type to use for which purpose. But as he went on, I turned to see Billy in the pillow corner, reading to the little ones. Liz and the others had novels open, fervently debating some aspect of them.

An ocean was between us now.

The kids settled at their desks again.

"Let's see," I said. "We're three chapters into our new novel."

"I don't mind starting over," Lee offered, smiling at Diamond and then at Ruby. The twins smiled back.

"Okay," I said. "That's very generous of you, Lee." I found

two additional copies of our book and we began reading aloud from the first page. At first, I listened to the girls as they read, paying attention to the words that slowed them down, asking them comprehension questions now and then. But I found it difficult to stay present.

Later, Julia came to ring the bell and lead kids out onto the green. Then it was just Billy and Liz and me inside and desperation seized my heart.

"We're going for a hike in the hills before dinner," Liz told me. "In case you want to come."

I turned away from her—toward the closets—and placed the day's materials back where they belonged. "No, that's okay," I said, still facing the shelves so she wouldn't see my face.

By the time I had finished putting everything away, I was alone.

I was bereft—wishing to be with Billy and Liz in the hills.

I craved escape—even if it was into something terrible.

But I would be strong and good and survive the despair. I would make one move and then another.

I soon found myself heading down the gravel road to the highway, the opposite direction of where Billy and Liz would be hiking. I felt drawn there, to the trail that Julia had shown me. Down the rocky cliffside I hiked. Through the wildflowers and the grasses, over the boulders and below to the pebbles and the sand. I found a spot to sit and watch the waves crash against the rocks. I thought of Julia, that first day, asking if I liked it. I still didn't know, but the loudness of it, the power of it, helped me remember where I was.

After sitting for a long time, I took off my shoes and rose to cross the small beach to stand in the froth.

A roaring wave, a shock of cold.

I stepped farther in. Stood until my feet were purple. Numb. The waves were growing high and strong—it was time to head back. I dried my feet with my socks and then pulled on my shoes.

I hiked to the highway on trembling legs, up the long gravel drive and through the gate. I stopped there, catching my breath against a boulder.

The air was colder, the sky quickly darkening. I passed the three cabins, lined up in their row, and entered the bathroom again. I chose not to turn on the lights. Stillness, all around me. The only sounds, those I made myself. The flush of the toilet, the stream of the faucet, my own hands rubbing together. I splashed water on my face. Placed my hands on my cheeks, then on my heart. Felt the rise and fall of my breath.

I returned to my cabin and lit a fire. I sat close, letting it warm me. And then a ghost darted past my window, bright as lantern light.

One afternoon, months after we'd moved to Blake's, I climbed up to the platform to look for Lorna and found she wasn't alone. I lowered the opera glasses. *Were my eyes playing tricks on me?* Lifted them to look again. Yes, it was true: a man, right beside her.

"You guys," I called out. I hurried back down the hill-side, rushing to show my mother and Blake. "My ghost! Lorna! Someone's with her."

Blake stood and turned around so he could see the street. There they were, plain as day. My ghost and a young man, taking her elbow, coaxing her back to the house.

Blake smiled, cocked his eyebrow. "Don't tell me you actually *believe* that poor old lady is a ghost."

It was like being pushed into a winter lake, sudden and heavy and cold.

"But . . . you said. You *told* me. Her name was Lorna and she died."

"How would I know what her name was?" He laughed. "She's some crazy old lady. A *ghost*," he said, and laughed harder. "Miriam, can you believe this?"

My mother shook her head. "Poor Mila," she said, but she was smiling, and soon she was laughing, too.

They laughed so hard, tears streamed down their faces. They laughed and laughed and laughed and laughed.

Alone in my cabin, I covered my ears.

I heard Blake leave later on and I knew my mother would come to me. "We got carried away," she told me. "We didn't mean anything by it."

"He does the same thing to you," I said.

"No."

"He does."

"No."

"The brains of teen moms don't fully develop? That isn't *true*."

"Honey, you don't know how these things work."

"I looked it up," I said. "He's *lying* to us."

"Honey," she said. "Sweetie pie. We got carried away. I thought it was a joke, but it was cruel to keep it going for so long. We—"

"Not *we*," I said. "Not *we*. Him."

"Blake wants the best for both of us. I thought I was doing a good job raising you. I really did. But he's helped me understand that all of this stuff—school and medicine and technology—it's all trying to control us. People aren't meant to live that way. There is an intuition—"

"Inside us! I know! I know what he says and I'm telling you it isn't true. He's controlling us. He's tricking us. He tricked me and he's tricking you, too."

"No."

"How many earrings have you lost?"

She bit her lip. "Come on, Mila."

"How many?"

"Nine," she whispered.

"Right," I said. "Nine. Like a person can even lose *nine* earrings."

I saw something then. A glimmer of openness. Like she wanted to believe me.

"I'll find them," I said.

"What do you mean?"

"I mean I think he has them. And if he has them, I'll find them. And if I find them, that means you have to believe me."

Each time Blake left, I sifted through his junk and his treasures, all of them wrapped in fabric and stored in various sizes of plastic bags. The opera glasses. The cologne. Bags full of shells—so many of them—the same kind he scattered through the dirt of his property. *The 4-Hour Workweek, Macbeth, The Artist's Way, Ulysses.* A small vase. A pair of girlish teacups. So, so many things.

And then—three days later, tucked into a slit in the side of his mattress, wrapped in a yellow scarf—nine single lost earrings.

My mother wept.

Later, we perched on the sunny platform, where we would be able to see him coming from a distance. We sat close enough to touch, but we weren't touching. I wanted to close the space between us, but I didn't know how. She loved me or she hated me for what I had just shown her. It was difficult to tell.

The sun beat down. I felt it on my hair, on my body.

"We have to leave," I said.

"And go where?"

"Grammy and Grandpa's."

"Honey," she said. A sob came from out of nowhere. "Honey, we can't. They died. Two months after we left. On the road back from Tahoe. A big rig."

Grammy's fingers on the piano keys.

Grandpa in front of the stove, stirring soup.

The safety of a warm bed.

Dancing.

"Oh," I said.

My hands went still. I understood then the trouble we were in. Why we had stayed for so long. Why they had never answered when I called them from the 7-Eleven pay phone that first winter when the cold nights left me aching and I thought I could count on them to save me. Instead, the phone had rung and rung and I could hear the ringing, again, as I sat with my mother and learned the truth.

And then I thought of something. "What about the house?" I asked. "Can we go back home?"

"The house is gone."

"*Gone?*"

"Sold."

"What happened to the money?"

She bit her lip. She didn't answer. And then I saw the master suite with its finished roof. Thought of its marble floor, its golden faucet. "Oh," I said again, and I tried not to hate her. "We can go somewhere else then," I said finally. "We can go to the police."

"And say what? *Oh, hi, officers. For nearly a year I've raised my daughter with no school and no toilet or shower or doctors.* Mila, they'll take you *away* from me. They'll lock me up. And he hasn't even committed a crime. There's nothing to go to them *for.*"

"Then we won't go to anybody," I said. "We'll get a motel room and we'll figure it out. Don't you have *any* money?"

"He takes it all. He keeps it for us."

I had searched everywhere there was to search, and I never found any money.

"You let him take everything," I said.

"I have no choice."

My fists clenched. I made myself breathe and loosened my fingers.

"So, what can we do?" I asked.

She didn't answer.

What can we do?

It was suspended in the air between us as the sun shone down. It was still there as we saw him in the distance, as he came nearer. It was there behind every word we spoke that evening. There in the chewing of crackers and the swallowing of water. There in the coffee and the tea. My mother's hand grazed mine as we did the dishes at the spigot and her touch asked the question. And still there was no answer.

All around us was dry grass, dry brush, the dry branches of dying trees.

All that time with Blake had turned her into someone else, and I thought of him, passed out and reeking in his bed, and could not understand how she could have stolen us from our life for *this*. Could not understand why she wanted to sleep with him instead of in the room we used to share, or stay up with him drinking coffee instead of herbal tea with honey in Grammy's floral-patterned easy chair. Could not understand why she'd chosen a life where the only times we really spoke to each other were when Blake was far away. Or why she rarely even hugged me anymore, rarely looked into my face.

Where was my mother?

"Oh, Mila," she said. "How will we get out of this?"

"We will," I said, though I didn't know the answer. "I know we will."

I was fearless, because she needed me to be.

Blake knew a lot of people. Most of them were transient. They'd come, pitch tents or sleep in the house on blankets, stay for a day or a week and move on. But Peggy and Matty lived close by and came over often. The four of them and whoever else was there would sit together by the firepit, talking late into the night, drinking beer or wine or liquor straight from the bottle. I usually stayed away, up on the platform near the top of the hill, or in my place at the far end of the house, reading by flashlight or trying to sleep. But not that night. My mother needed me; I could feel it. So I made my own place by the fire.

"Oh, look. The kid is joining us," Peggy said when she saw me. "You're usually off hiding somewhere."

I shrugged. She cocked her head, assessing me.

"You must have been a baby when you had her," she said to my mother.

"Fifteen."

"Where's the dad?" Matty asked, popping the cap off another beer.

"*You* tell them," my mother said, smiling at me. I had been quiet, on the periphery. She was inviting me in. So I told them about the party and the movie and the conversation that followed. I pushed aside the ache over my grandparents, how I would never see them again—that wasn't what this was about. This was about my mother and me.

I told them, "She knew he wouldn't be a good father, so she made a decision."

"Men," Matty said. "Who needs them? Right, ladies?"

Peggy laughed too loudly. But I couldn't tell whether Matty was being self-deprecating or whether he was being mean. I didn't know what to say or what to do with my face. I was glad for the darkness, sheltered by it.

The fire crackled and danced.

"Decision," Blake said. "*Decision*. That is an interesting word."

Peggy giggled. I didn't know why.

"It implies power," Blake said. "Power that you didn't have, Miriam."

My mother looked down. I couldn't see her face.

"I don't know if it *implies* anything," Peggy said. "It seems pretty simple. She could have told him she was pregnant. She decided not to."

"Now *that*," Blake said, pointing at Peggy, "is an accurate statement. But it is not what Miriam and Mila are trying to convey. Their little story, in the way they have framed it, is that Miriam somehow possessed the power to determine whether or not this boy would have *the privilege* of being Mila's father. It's classic Miriam, really.

So typical. She's such a *treasure*. Her daughter is so *perfect*. How *fortunate* that boy would have been to find out that some girl he fucked at a party was carrying his child. Surely, he would have been so eager to give up his whole future for a minimum-wage job and a life spent in service to the two of them."

My mother still looked down. Her shoulders shook, and I couldn't tell if she was laughing or crying.

Maybe it was both.

But me? I took Blake's words and I blew them apart. I stripped away every mean thing until, sitting under the stars with the fire dancing across our faces, with Peggy looking blankly into the flames and Matty halfheartedly chuckling, with my mother maybe-laughing, maybe-crying, hidden from me in the dark, all I heard was one thing.

She thought I was perfect.

On my fourteenth birthday, my mother took her tips from the previous night's shift and bought me a blue sweater at the mall. She wrapped it with a bow and gave it to me while Blake grilled cheap cuts of steak to go with the nightly vegetables.

I put it right on, found it so warm and soft that I wanted to leave early and fall asleep in it. But Blake told me to wait.

"I have a special something of my own for you," he said. He handed me a small box, the kind he so often handed to my mother. I saw her eyes darken in confusion. I opened the lid and there was a pair of earrings. Gold. He only ever bought my mother silver.

I couldn't look at her face.

"My ears aren't pierced," I told him.

"No time like the present," Blake said. "A woman of fourteen should wear earrings. I bought some rubbing alcohol for the occasion. Wouldn't want an infection like your mother keeps getting. All it takes is a little hygiene."

"Blake," my mother said. "There's a place I know. They have a special tool for it. A gun. Let's take her there."

He doused the earrings in alcohol, poured more on his fingers and rubbed my earlobes.

"It will be fun!" my mother said. "We'll go as a family. It's a special gun. It works so quick. *Blake.*"

But he didn't listen. He stabbed the earrings into my earlobes. One sharp pain and then another, and then hours of throbbing until my mother crept to my bed with two empty pillowcases and ice in a paper cup from the convenience store. She split the ice between the pillowcases. She had me lie on my back so she could press the ice against both ears at the same time.

Stars flashed in front of my eyes. My earlobes throbbed. I was on the floor of my cabin, arms wrapped around my knees.

One breath and then another, I told myself.

I made it to the door and pushed it open, stumbled into the evening, the sun just setting. Billy and Liz were leaving the second cabin.

"Walk over with us?" Liz asked.

"Where?"

Billy cocked his head. "The house. For dinner. Are you okay?"

"Oh," I said. "Dinner."

Liz took a few steps toward me. "Hey," she said, squinting. "What happened to your ears?"

"My ears?" I touched one and then the other. When I lowered my hand to look, blood was on my fingertips. "Oh," I said. "Yes. The earrings. I . . . He pierced them." My head was heavy, my mind swimming. "I don't think I should go to dinner," I said. "Not yet. You go ahead, though."

I turned away from them. Something was on my doorstep. A little brown box. I picked it up, but waited until Billy's and Liz's steps faded in the distance to open it. When I knew I was alone, I pulled off the string and lifted the top.

A pair of earrings. Emerald studs.

The next time Blake's friends came to drink and talk by the fire, I chose to stay away. I lay up the hill in my sleeping bag, with a novel and a flashlight. I was lost in the world of my book, so I didn't notice when Blake went to bed, too drunk to socialize any longer. Didn't notice when Peggy tried to stand but fell forward, rose again to find her sweater in flames. I didn't see her tear off the sweater or hurl it away, into some brush.

It was California in the summertime. The hill was ablaze in seconds.

My mother screamed and I sat up. There it was, below me, orange and white and hot. "Mila!" she yelled. "Blake's inside! Wake him up!" And then she and Peggy and Matty and whoever else was there that night catapulted down the hill to the street, away from the flames.

I rushed down the hillside, slipped, and tore my only pair of jeans. And then I was on the foundation, pushing open the door to Blake's room.

"Mila, I found you!"

Lee was trotting toward me from across the green. I dropped the box behind me. I didn't want him to see it. "Liz said you might still be here. Dinner's on the table."

"Already?" I asked.

"Yeah, the sky's dark. Don't you see?"

I looked up. "Yes, I do."

"You don't feel well. It's the ghosts, right?"

"I don't know. I think I might be . . . I think I need to . . ."

"Just come have dinner and then you can go to bed early. Aren't you hungry?"

"I'm hungry," I said.

"Here," he said. "We'll walk slowly. I'll hold your hand."

Most everyone was already seated when I slid onto the edge of a bench. Dinner looked nourishing—butternut squash soup with olive oil and basil and cracked black pepper, warm bread, and salad—and I was suddenly ravenous.

Emma was next to me. "Are you feeling okay?" she asked.

"I'm a little tired," I said.

"You seem kind of . . . *off*."

"I just . . . haven't been sleeping."

"Okay."

She handed me the salad bowl, her thin gold band catching the light.

I filled my plate with the garden lettuces and carrots and radishes and chives, smelled tarragon and the tang of apple cider vinegar. Julia set a bowl of soup at my place, followed by the bread and the fresh butter.

I wanted to be full, to be comforted. Billy was across the table with the little ones. Liz was in a corner, her face in shadow.

I took a spoonful of soup, expecting the familiar sweetness of it, but all I tasted was smoke. Maybe Terry had tried a new recipe. Maybe he'd charred the squash before pureeing it. I glanced around the table. The little ones were spooning big bites of soup into their mouths, dipping bread into their bowls and chewing. Liz took a spoonful. I saw her savor it, dip her spoon in again.

I would eat the salad instead. But despite the crunch of the lettuce and the scent of its dressing, it tasted burnt, too. I forced myself to swallow; my stomach churned. I gulped a sip of my water, but it didn't wash the taste away. Instead, it somehow made it worse.

"Oh my God," Jackson said. "Liz, tell everyone what you taught us today."

Liz made some kind of joke and everyone laughed and she started telling her story.

The bread and the butter. They would be fine, and

enough to fill me up. The butter melted as I spread it on the still-warm slice. I bit in, hungry and desperate, but it was worse than the others had been. It was ash in my mouth. Smoldering, sickening. I felt the press of memory.

Not here, I thought. *Not now.*

I was on the foundation, pushing the door to Blake's room open.

No.

There I was, at the table with everyone.

There Blake was, on the mattress. He was shifting a little bit. Maybe some distant part of him smelled smoke and sensed danger.

Even in the urgency, time seemed to stop.

"Save him!" my mother screamed from below.

I stood in the doorway to his room. He sprawled on his new bed, the bed where he fucked my mother, the bed he bought with my grandparents' money.

I could wake him.

Morning would come.

He would rise and devour us again.

Lies and tricks. The way he took her from me and kept taking and taking. My ghost—he took her, too. And he hurt us on purpose. And he poisoned everything good—the

California poppies, the hours my mother spent with me, even the story of us.

My heart pounded rage instead of blood. At first there was a stab in my chest, a blindness. And then my vision returned. The flames crept closer.

I still had time to save him. All I had to do was throw something in his direction. Kick him. *Scream.*

He may have been a monster in the daylight, but at that moment he was only a man, asleep. Flesh and bones and a beating heart. Hair and clothing. Lungs that would fill with smoke.

The flames caught the drapes above the bed.

All I had to do was warn him.

Fire engulfed the blankets. I could scream, and he would wake.

And then the flames found his hair, his clothing. I saw him stir. I could have saved him, but I made a choice.

Bread and butter and ash in my mouth.

I gagged and the food flew out, onto my plate, but what landed didn't look like bread at all. It was powdery and black.

The sight of it made me heave. I vomited right there, onto the floor of Terry and Julia's house—not food but ash—wet and clumpy and vile. Like our blackened, ruined things when all of it was over, drenched and then forgotten.

I sprang from the bench, holding my stomach, flooded with shame. *How could I be so disgusting?* Turned toward me were so many faces—Liz and Billy and Lee, Terry and Julia, Emma and Hunter and Jackson, Darius and Blanca and Mackenzie and James, Diamond and Ruby—all of them, horrified.

"I'm so sorry," I sobbed. "I didn't . . ."

I stepped out of the doorway as the room filled with smoke and fire.

"I couldn't . . ."

I turned from him right before the walls crashed in.

"I don't know what's happening," I said, and my stomach heaved again, and I had to cover my mouth.

Julia was beside me now, her arm tightening around my waist.

I left him there—a man—to burn to death.

"Come with me," Julia said.

And I let her lead me away.

An hour later, I emerged from the downstairs bathroom, the taste of ash still faintly in my mouth despite the new toothbrush and paste Julia had given me. I had brushed twice, scrubbed my tongue, but it wouldn't go away.

Still, I was calmer. I was clean, my skin warm from the bath Julia had drawn for me, scented by the lavender-and-rosemary bath salts she'd made. The kitchen floor had been washed and the house was quiet. Terry sat alone at the table.

He looked up as I crossed the floor.

"Let's sit," he said, and we went into the living room together. I sat on the easy chair and he took a place across from me on the sofa. He clasped his hands. "So," he said. "The fire?"

I nodded. I wanted it to make sense—all of it. The scent of the coins on my hand, the cut on my foot, the poppies and the earrings and the ash . . . but the harder I grasped for logic, the more clouded everything became. I would return to this one thing, Terry's question. The fire.

"Why—" I started. "Why would it be *inside* me?"

He started to speak and then stopped himself. "I wish I had the answers," he said. But his words didn't feel right. Or, more than that, they didn't feel like *enough*.

"Why do you bring us here?" I asked.

"The farm healed Julia and me. We were lost when we came here. We found our way back to each other, to ourselves. It's healed so many people. It can do that for *you*, too. If you let it."

I shook my head. Looked at my hands, clasped together on my lap.

"I feel like it's destroying me," I said.

He turned away from me, toward the dark window. I

did the same, and saw our reflection: Terry and me, together. No longer strangers. And then I heard footsteps from their bedroom. Julia was here now, hair in a braid, dressed in flannel for bed.

"How are you feeling?" she asked. The concern in her eyes, the way she looked at me so carefully—she wanted me here. I was wrapped in the midnight-blue robe she had laid out for me the hour before. Before she'd left me to undress, she'd kissed me on the cheek, not minding the ash-vomit in my hair.

"I don't know," I said.

"You'll get through this, Mila," Terry said.

"Trust us," Julia said.

I wished they could know how difficult it was. How near to impossible. Wished I could hand them my memories, intact, so they could see the earrings and the shells and the ways that I had been tricked. So they could see Lorna and how purely I'd believed in her. *Oh,* they would say. *I see.*

And they would tell me everything about the ghosts and the farm. Offer answers to all the questions I didn't know how to ask. They'd know what was going on inside of me. They'd tell me about Lee, and the field. And I would be strong enough to hear the truth, as much as it might hurt me. Once they had been completely honest, I would trust them forever.

"Why did Samantha run away?" I asked.

I thought of the walk Julia and I had taken on my first afternoon at the farm. *People need to know where they fit in in the world*, she'd said. I wanted to know why I was here.

Julia closed her eyes, rubbed the space between her brows with her long, graceful fingers. Her nails were short, dark around the edges with dirt that never washed away. Terry turned his gaze up from the floor, looked straight into my eyes.

"Everyone who joins our family has suffered. Suffered terribly. Some are more resilient than others. We try to choose wisely, but some won't ever find peace here." He ran his hands over his head, dropped them in his lap. "Maybe the farm makes it worse for those people. That possibility weighs on me."

I nodded. I understood something of what he was saying, but I didn't know which type of person I was. I didn't know if my fate was decided. Was the farm cradling me and showing me the way, or was it bringing it all back just to haunt me? I saw the good and the breathtaking and the bad and the rotten. I saw all of it. But a voice, even then, was whispering that it was one. No parsing to be done. Revelation and obscurity, terror and power, beauty and revulsion, joy and shame—all of it together in its tangle. Horrible and lovely. Mine always to keep.

I stood. "I'm going to bed."

"Mila," Terry said. "Wait. I've been meaning to talk to

you about the other night. I don't always know how to do this. I don't always get it right."

I was listening to him, but I was also looking out the window, toward my cabin. I was ready to go.

"Mila," he said again. "Will you look at me?"

I did, and I saw more in his face than I ever had. I saw how he could be gentle and he could be stern. I saw that he was not only one kind of man. Warmth rushed into his eyes. *Why?* I wondered. And then I realized that the warmth was for me.

"You, my friend, came to us with an openness that stunned me. That first night at the piano. The way you listen to everyone, anytime one of us is talking. You notice people. You know what is needed and you do it. Whenever some hidden mess is tidied, some forgotten task completed, I think to myself, *That was Mila.* And even if you hadn't done any of those things, I would care for you anyway."

I nodded, a storm swelling in my chest.

"There will be a night, some night, I am *sure* of it, when the mystery of all of this won't be so difficult anymore. None of us will *ever* understand all of it, but you will not be in the dark."

I wanted his words to be true. I tried to believe him.

"I have a hard time with people in pain," he said. "Especially children. And I was not patient with you; I was not kind. I was worried for Lee, but that's a poor excuse. Not a day goes by that I don't, also, worry for you."

"What for?"

He gestured to the window, his attention on me unwavering.

"I need you to be brave," he said. "I need you to face her, even though it hurts."

I broke our gaze. It was too much.

"May I walk you across the field?" Julia asked.

"I'll be all right," I said. "But thank you."

I tied the robe tighter as I stepped into the night. A small ghost was playing with some other ghost children on the green, so I chose to walk the path. The moon was full and huge in the sky. My feet crunched the gravel. Then two ghost girls, holding hands, appeared together out of the fog. *Twins.* My breath caught but I kept walking, too weary to think of what it might mean. I would make it to my cabin, and I would try not to think too much, try to fall fast asleep, and the sun would rise on a new day. Toward me came another glow, this one leaping and spinning. She got so close to me—I had to cover my eyes—but then she was gone.

AS THE NEXT DAY WORE ON, the evening's approach made my heart race. I didn't want to be alone in my cabin, so I set out down the path and out the gate, as I had with Julia on my first full day at the farm and so many times with Billy and Liz in those magical, fleeting weeks when we were friends.

I followed the path to the bluff, hiked part of the way down. It was late October. It was cold. No one was out here. Below me were rocks and ocean and there was no reason to be afraid. I sat, arms around my knees, ready to watch the sunset. But I saw someone, then, far below me, close to the water. I saw someone and then saw him more clearly.

"Lee!" I called out. I waved. He didn't wave back. What was he doing, so close to the water, all alone and so late in the day? I rose and began the descent, and as I got closer I could make out his expression. He looked the way he had that first school day.

Pale and trembling.

As I neared, I thought I saw him begin to move and then

change his mind, as though held back by some force not his own.

"What are you doing down here?" I asked when I reached him. "You know you shouldn't be here alone. You shouldn't be here at *all* this late."

He shook his head. He wouldn't meet my gaze. His fists were clenched, hiding something.

"What is this?" I asked, trying to keep my voice steady and kind. I could tell he was afraid, but I was not someone to be afraid of. Maybe once, but that was so long ago. That was in another life.

He shook his head.

"Show me," I said. But by then I was able to see what he was holding. I could see, also, that his pockets were full. I didn't understand, at first, why he'd be hiding them from me. And then I realized.

My vision darkened. My face grew hot.

"*Show me,*" I said again.

He unclenched his fists and let their contents fall.

"And your pockets?"

He emptied his pockets. More fell.

Shells. So many of them.

I wanted to believe I had misunderstood. That the shells had nothing to do with what I told him that night in the living room, when we sat on the sofa with the fire crackling, and he told me he was afraid and I confessed that I was, too. But there was no ambiguity in his guilty expression, no doubt in the hunch of his shoulders, his shame over being found out.

I brought my hands to my face and covered my eyes. I couldn't look at him. The waves crashed in. I wanted to be taken out to sea. The black, freezing depths of it. The pain of this, gone.

I lowered my hands.

"You tricked me," I said.

"But—"

"The poppies?"

He nodded. "But I didn't know—"

"*The earrings?*" I shrieked.

"Yes, but—"

I pushed my hands over my ears. I didn't want to hear what else he might say. It was ruined, it was gone. All that I thought we had shared.

We shouldn't have been here on these rocks at twilight. I knew that. And I knew that the rage rising within me was out of my control. It would choke out all the remaining light. I was rotten, I was wretched, I was bad. How stupid to think I could ever be good.

I thought Lee loved me, but he didn't. I thought I was worthy of his love, but I had to turn from him and go.

So I didn't let him say anything else. Instead I ran back up the rocks, the ocean loud behind me, the tide creeping ever higher. I expected Lee to catch me because he was such a fast runner, so I pushed myself to outrun him for his own sake. I was not to be trusted. I was a danger to him. I was a fourteen-year-old with a grievance and dry brush and a flame—the same girl I was then—falling for the same tricks.

But when I reached the top of the bluff, he still hadn't caught up to me.

I didn't hear his footsteps in the distance.

I stopped.

Still no footsteps behind me. And then I thought of how Lee had tried to run at first but hadn't. How he had been standing strangely and so very still.

I turned and looked to where the bluff met the sky. I made my way to the edge. There he was, in the same place, the water up to his knees now, even when the waves were out. He was bent over, struggling.

He was stuck.

And that night at the skeleton house came back to me, once again. The flames creeping closer as I stood in the doorway. The choice that I made. For a horrifying moment atop the bluff, Lee wasn't Lee to me at all. He was just another person who had tricked me on purpose, another person who'd hurt me. And I could make the same choice a second time and be rid of him, too.

But in the split second that I thought of leaving him there, a cry rose up from inside of me. I had made Lee a promise never to leave him. I had told him I'd protect him, whatever the cost. And, more than any of that, I *loved* him.

I moved as fast as I could back down the bluff. I almost flew. And then we were face-to-face again, the water up to Lee's waist now, and he was saying, "Help me. My foot."

I held my breath and went under, felt the shock of the freezing cold water on my face, in my eyes. His ankle was stuck between two rocks. I tried to move one, but it wouldn't budge. I surfaced. A wave was coming, growing and growing until I saw it would crash over us. "Hold on to me," I said. "As tight as you can. Don't let go even if it hurts."

We held on to each other as the wave crashed over our heads. It drenched us and washed away again. The water was up to *my* waist now, up to Lee's chest.

I plunged under again and wrapped my hand around his ankle. I got a better hold this time and pulled as hard as I could—enough for Lee's foot to come loose. Just as I came up for air, another wave covered us. It *wanted* us. I held my breath and held on to Lee's chest, his arms around my neck, and I felt myself be swept away.

And I felt that we were still together.

We reached the surface, both of us sputtering, coughing. He tried to break and swim for shore but I held his hand. "Don't struggle," I called out. "Just give in. It will bring us back."

And Julia was right. It did.

On the rocks again, above the water, my clothes clung to my body, heavy and cold. Lee's foot was blue, blood pouring from it. I smelled metal and salt. Took off my shirt and tied it around his foot as tightly as I could. I pulled my soaked sweater back on and had him climb onto my back and loop his arms around my shoulders and—*somehow*—I got us back up the bluff, and back home.

They had not been worried about us. Later, Julia would tell me that when they noticed Lee's absence, they also made note of mine. They guessed that we had been out together—pupil and teacher, brother and sister—enjoying the twilight.

So they were not expecting anything unusual when I burst through the door with Lee on my back, both of us soaking wet, blood dripping from Lee's foot onto my leg and down, so that I tracked red footprints through the kitchen.

"Oh my God," Terry said and rushed toward me to take Lee. What lightness, to have him lifted from me after carrying him so far. Julia and Liz rose from the table, shock on their faces.

Julia rushed to the telephone while Liz grabbed towels from the linen closet. She wrapped one towel around me and the other around Lee as Terry removed my shirt from Lee's foot. Lee moaned as he pulled it off. I tried to watch, but all I could see was Lee's pockets full of shells, his look of being found out, and I had to close my eyes.

"*Fuck*," Terry said. I'd never heard him swear, never heard his voice so low.

I opened my eyes to the bleeding gash across Lee's ankle.

"What happened?" Terry asked.

"My foot got stuck in the rocks," Lee said. "I shouldn't have been down there."

"You went by yourself?"

"Yes."

"*Lee*," he admonished.

"Sorry," Lee said, his voice so small.

"Hold on." Terry headed to the bathroom. "I'm getting the gauze."

"You're still shaking," Liz said to me. "We need to get you warmed up."

"I just want to go to bed," I said.

I stood up.

"Take care of her," Terry said to Liz. "Watch over her. Okay?" He was taking a half dozen items from a huge first aid kit.

"Of course," Liz said.

I started to stand but Lee pulled my arm. "Wait." He grabbed me around the neck and raised his mouth to my ear. "The poppies were a present. I didn't know anything then. Remember? I was just so happy you were here. But the earrings, the shells . . . I thought you *wanted* me to. I thought it would help . . . like you said."

"*Help?*" I asked him, pulling away.

He nodded. He tightened his grip, drew me even closer until I felt his breath on my cheek, his lips touching my ear.

"Help you not be afraid."

It all came back to me.

The fairy tales. The drawing of my ghost. The words I'd spoken as I tried to help him: *We have to face the things that scare us. It might be the only way to stop being afraid.* It all came back and I understood and I had to leave the kitchen.

I couldn't stay a moment longer in the house, but once I was crossing the field with Liz by my side, my legs weakened and I had to lean against her for support. I let her lead me to our bathroom instead of to my cabin. I didn't even know what I wanted, anyway.

She turned the water on as hot as it would go. I was soaking wet and shaking and I didn't know what to do. My arms were limp at my sides. I had never been so tired.

"I've done such terrible things," I sobbed. "I did such a terrible thing."

"No," she said. "You just *saved* Lee."

"I'm not talking about that." I was sobbing so hard I could barely breathe, but the words spilled out anyway.

"I'm going to help you undress," Liz said. "Okay?"

"Okay."

Off came the soaking wet sweater.

In my first foster homes, the ones I was placed in before Amy and Jonathan's, I waited to feel guilty. I waited to feel ashamed. When the feelings didn't come, I researched what happens to people when they die in a fire, how their bodies shut down. But despite the horrible things I found, I was still relieved that Blake was dead. I was still all fury and no regret. Still trembling with how he had destroyed us.

I would hate him forever. I would think of how he burned and it would not shame me.

But what kind of monster did that make me?

"I knew he would die," I said. "I knew he would die. I knew he would die, and I left him there because of it, and he was burned alive."

I was naked now, shivering.

"*Shhhh*," Liz said. "*Sh-shhh*," she said again. "Here, climb in. I'll help you."

"I'm bad," I said. "I'm dangerous. I can't be trusted. She told me to save him but I killed him instead."

She took my arm and led me to the tub. My whole body shook and I didn't know if it was from the cold or the betrayal or the way I had been gutted. The way I had gutted myself. I had confessed, had said plainly what I'd done for the first time, but nothing had changed. Not even the way Liz looked at me was different. Her face was all concern and I didn't deserve it.

She helped me to step into the hot water. My body didn't know what to feel. I lowered myself into it. I put my face in my hands.

"I thought he was haunting me," I said.

"Maybe he was."

"No. It was Lee."

"Lee?"

"He tricked me. Or I tricked him. I don't know. I almost left him there."

I saw it again—Lee on the rocks, throwing the shells down, his foot caught and not calling for help. He would have died. How could I have harbored any doubt? Lee had my heart.

But what had I been doing to him all this time?

I had told him too much. I had let him take care of me. I had wrapped him up in my fears, in trying to fix me, and he had almost died trying to give me what I needed.

"Lee," I said. "Lee, I'm sorry. Lee, I'm sorry."

"Mila," Liz said. "*Shhhh,*" she said. But I kept repeating it over and over again. I tried to stop but I couldn't.

Lee was right. I had wanted to be haunted. Had needed to be.

"I'm sorry," I said again.

Liz's clothes dropped to the ground. I felt her step into the water. It rose to my shoulders as she sunk in behind me. She took my body in her arms and pulled me toward her, and it was only then that I stopped shaking.

"It doesn't matter what you did," she told me, my back against her breasts, her arms around my chest, her cheek against my cheek. "You're here now and it's over."

"Lee, I'm so sorry."

"*Sh-shhh*," she said.

Across the field, the house's lights were on. Eventually, I heard the crunch of wheels on the gravel drive and knew it was Dr. Cole's wagon. I understood, then, that Lee would be all right. No long trip down Highway One to the hospital. Everything he needed could be done here. Lee got twenty-three stitches, a dose of pain medication, and a mug of steamed milk. Julia, worried about secondary drowning, would carry her rocking chair from the little ones' room and spend the night next to him, watching his chest rise and fall.

By the time Dr. Cole crossed the field to find me, Liz had me dry and in pajamas, lying in my bed with the fire crackling.

"How are you feeling?" he asked. I didn't know how to answer, so said nothing. He crossed the cabin and placed a hand on my shoulder. His voice soft, he said, "This will be quick." I closed my eyes at the cold press of metal on my chest. He listened to my lungs and my heart.

"Good girl," he said when it was over.

I slept in late on Sunday, woke to light through the curtains. Liz and Billy were already at the market, probably on their second cups of coffee, were probably counting change and chatting with customers. I buried my head in the pillow and fell back to sleep.

A couple hours later, Julia brought me eggs and tea and tangerines on a tray. She kissed me on the head and didn't make me talk to her.

In the late afternoon, Terry came with bread and soup.

"How is Lee?" I asked him.

"He's doing all right." Terry sat at the edge of my bed. He took my hand. "Thanks to you," he said, but I didn't deserve it. He must have sat with me and held my hand until I fell asleep again, because I don't remember him leaving.

———

Lee and I were given the next day off from lessons. I slept as long as I could because I didn't know what else to do. I didn't know if Lee would even want to see me. But in the late morning, when I went into the kitchen, he was there at the table. He'd been waiting for me. I filled the kettle and lit the stove. I spooned tea leaves into a strainer. I waited for the water to boil and for the tea to steep. Only then was I strong enough to face him.

I sat next to him at the table.

I looked at his face.

I took his hand in my hand.

"Lee," I said. "I'm sorry."

I said it without crying. I said it for him and not for myself.

He rested his head against my shoulder, the best gift I had ever been given.

take me back

THERE WAS A TIME THEN, after what we all came to call "the accident," when things went more or less back to normal. I returned to the schoolhouse to teach the twins. They were all cooperation, all compliments, but all I wanted was Lee. When he did come back for lessons, I had to keep myself from staring as he read aloud and wrote his numbers, as he moved with a limp to the closets and told us he was fine. We had survived, I reminded myself when I felt my chest tighten. We had been in trouble, but we were okay now.

Dr. Cole came by once in a while to check on Lee and rule out infection, and then, two weeks after the accident, he arrived to pull out the stitches. I sat with Lee and held his hand while Dr. Cole snipped and pulled and dabbed the drops of blood with alcohol. "I wish I'd had the dissolving stuff that night," he said to Lee. "I'm sorry about that, young man."

"It's okay," Lee told him, trying to sound strong. But he

squeezed my hand hard and I wished that he would squeeze even harder. I wished for him to break my bones.

I had been haunting myself as punishment, I supposed. But it was difficult, when ghosts were everywhere, to figure out what was real and what was imagined. The glowing figures, the shadows, the ghost at the piano, the blood on my foot and my earlobes . . . they'd all been real. Proof that *something* was out there, even if it had never been Blake. Something was there, just not what I'd thought.

I started to pay closer attention. For the first time, I really *looked* at the ghosts, one by one. The little ghost Lee had cradled that night never returned, but when I pictured him in my memory I saw how *like* Lee he was. The same sweet little nose, the same shape of his mouth. The rest of the ghosts were unfamiliar to me, except for the twins, of course. I watched them hold hands from my cabin window one night. Even at a distance, I could tell which girl was Diamond and which was Ruby.

And then came the night when Terry and I were at the kitchen window, and the dancing ghost appeared on the green. A feeling swept over me—a dizziness, a shortness of breath—and I began to turn away.

But Terry took hold of my arm to stop me. "Remember what I told you," he said. And so, I looked.

She was close enough that I could see her long hair, the girlish curves of her body, her calves, and her bare feet.

I willed her not to come closer, but I also willed my fear away.

Liz was there when I stepped out, perched on the steps right outside the mudroom, drinking tea. "May I sit with you?" I asked, and she scooted over to make space beside her.

She offered me her mug and I sipped. Peppermint. It brought me back to the first time I met Nick, when he told me about the teaching and told me about the market but didn't tell me anything at all. Still, once again, the tea made me feel like I was starting over. Made me feel like maybe starting over once again was still possible.

I saw figures in the distance, near the schoolhouse. Two adults and two children. "Is that Billy and Julia?" I asked. Liz nodded. "With the twins?"

"Yes," she said.

As my eyes adjusted to the dark, I saw that Billy held Ruby's hand and Julia held Diamond's. They meandered down the drive, pointing out stars in the sky. I imagined Billy identifying the constellations, Julia telling the myths.

"I'll tell you now," Liz said. "If you still want me to."

I knew what she wanted to say. I nodded.

"All right." She gazed over the field. She set her mug on the step. With a steady voice, she said, "I was six years old the first time my mother left me. I was in first grade. A nice family wanted to adopt me, but my mom kept coming back, so I was moved around, from house to house. Every year or so, she would show up again, tell me that she loved me, and tell me she was fighting for me. As soon as I believed her, she would disappear again."

I took her hand. Two streaks ran down her cheeks, aglow in the moonlight. With my other hand, as tenderly as I could, I wiped them away.

"And then," she said quietly, "I turned eighteen."

I ached with recognition. "It would have been easier to be hopeless," I said.

"Yes." She took in a breath. Let it out. "No one should suffer from that kind of hope."

By the time I crossed the field back to my cabin, I'd said good night to Ruby and Diamond and Billy and Julia. Liz had gone to bed and I thought all the ghosts had, too. I took off my shoes and turned on Billie Holiday. I built my fire and sat in front of it, letting it warm me. And then I went to shut the curtain and turn out the light.

Something was on the field, glowing in the dark. The fog was thick, so I couldn't see her clearly, but the way she moved was enough for me to know it was her.

My ghost, waiting for me.

I knew it was time, finally, to greet her.

I slipped on my shoes and opened my door and then I was out in the misty cold.

She was in the middle of the field, dancing, just as she had been on my first night. But as I neared her, there was more. I heard music. A piano. Something light and fast. And then that song ended and the ghost closed her eyes and waited for a new song to begin. I knew it from its first few notes. I knew it from my Billie Holiday record, and I knew it from my piano playing, and I knew it from farther back. And when she began to dance again, I found that I remembered every motion before she made it. When her arms were going to rise, when she was going to spin and leap. I remembered the dance because I had been taught the same one and had practiced for hours, less out of duty than for the joy it brought me. When she was finished, the music stopped, too, and she walked toward me.

Here it was—what I had been trying for so long not to see.

She had my face. My body. Not as it was as I stood there, but as it had been before I left my grandparents' house. She was me, at thirteen years old, suspended in time at the moment when I had last been whole.

We stepped closer. I even recognized her dress—white with pale blue lace trim. My grandmother had sewn it for my recital. We were face-to-face now. Here she was, the girl who I had been.

She was so lovely.

She didn't know what was to come.

"You recognize me," she said, and her voice was sweet as birdsong, her smile bright.

"Yes," I told her. "I do."

"Took you long enough."

"I know," I said. "But here I am."

"Dance with me," she said.

"No." I shook my head. "I can't."

"Come on! You *have* to. I've been trying to get this last move right. You have to teach me."

She extended her arm to one side and waited.

I didn't want to. I didn't want to.

She was still waiting, arm extended.

And then I changed my mind.

I *wanted* to.

I mirrored her position. She pointed her right foot and I pointed my left. Together, our arms rose over our heads and our feet lifted off the ground. Together, we bent forward and spun a half turn, and my hair in the wind, the movement I made, brought back my life.

A leap. *Look how precious you were.* A spin. *How worthy of love you were.* A dip. *Look at your heart, intact.* Reach to the sky. *What a miracle it was.* Swoop to the grass. *How steadily it beat for the people you loved.*

We danced, together, in the dark field of music. We

danced with the fog all around us, my feet landing heavy on the grass, hers weightless. We danced until I lost my breath and had to stop. I watched her as she spun, tears streaming down my face, side aching with the effort of the movements, heart aching with memory. I watched her and I thought that of the two of us, *I* was surely the ghost. I was the faded one, and she was still vibrant and young, full of abandon and light.

But also: I was the one with a heartbeat, with a body that made me stop and rest, with time that would someday run out. Of the two of us, I was the one with a responsibility to the world, so I needed to wake myself up.

"Mila," I said to her. And I thought she didn't hear me at first, but then her movements began to change and slowly, slowly, she came to the end of her dance.

"What do we do now?" I asked her.

I was surprised, at first, by her sadness. I had thought she felt only delight—but sadness, of course, was a feeling all of us have always known. Was a feeling I had known, even before everything else.

"Oh, Mila," she said. "You have to take me back."

"How do I do that? Grammy and Grandpa are dead. Our mother is gone. There's nowhere to take you back *to*."

"No," she said, and pressed her hand like Dr. Cole's stethoscope against my heart. "*You* have to take me back."

"Oh. When?"

Not soon, I hoped.

Maybe we could spend a few more nights together. I would never look away again. We could dance this way on other nights. The farm was full of ghosts, so surely, *surely*, she could stay awhile longer.

"Now," she said. "If you're ready."

"I'm not."

"But you've seen me. I've been waiting so long. You have to take me back."

"What about all the others?" I asked. "So many have stayed."

"They were *abandoned*. You can't leave me that way." She searched my eyes. "It's good to understand," she said.

"I know."

"So, you're ready?"

I thought of how, when Lee had cried out, he'd had the others with him. Had their comfort and their care. But he was still a child and I was grown up. I was no one's responsibility anymore. Still, how I wished Liz could be there to hold me. How I wished for Billy's explanations, and for Julia's arm in mine, and for Terry's kindness, his insistence that I belonged.

I was alone. I was frightened.

If only she had never worked in that diner. If only I had been enough. If they'd never let me go, and I had spent the next months safe, practicing the piano, missing my mother, and I had not run out of quarters at the pay phone, and they had not died and left me forever. If not for the nine lost earrings. If not for the late nights by the fire. If not for my wild recklessness, my desperate choice.

"This will hurt," she said.

"It's okay," I lied. "I'm ready."

She took my hands and stepped in closer, touched her forehead to my forehead, her chest to my chest. I had just found her. I wasn't ready to say goodbye. The night was blue gray and foggy. Cold and damp. But together we were sharp. Bright. The pain seized me at the heart, radiated outward.

None of us were supposed to be living there, not even Blake. Even if you own the property, no one can live in a skeleton house. Plus, everyone Blake knew was running from something, so the rest of them fled and it was only my mother and me, watching the firefighters at work and giving statements. Only the two of us, standing down the street as the hillside burned. Only me petting her hair when Blake was pronounced dead at the scene and she howled at the moon like the wolves that they were.

Plenty of people came out of their houses, craned their necks to see. The firefighters made quick work of it and the police questioned onlookers and we heard strangers saying that they never liked what was going on over there. How people came and went. We heard some-one say something about a woman and a girl, but no one knew it was us.

We kept watching even after the fire was out, after the examiner came, until Blake's body, zipped in a bag, was loaded into the back of a medical transport van. And then even that was gone.

What was left was the blackened ground and the toxic burnt-tarp smell and the ash in the air. And her, and me, and the sun beginning its rise in the distance.

She cried and I didn't. She covered her mouth, maybe because of the smoke and maybe because of the horror.

"We loved him so much," she said. "He took such good care of us for so long, and now he's gone."

But he was never good to us. I never loved him. I searched her eyes for the truth. *Where was my mother?* Felt the weight of another trick being played on me.

The next night we fell asleep in a shelter. Two cots side by side in a large room full of sleeping women and girls. I woke to her shaking my shoulder in the dark.

She was my mother. It was the two of us again. Once, I'd been smaller than a speck of dust but she'd loved me.

"Why didn't you save him?" she asked.

"I saved *us*," I said.

Her face crumpled in pain, in fury.

She grabbed me by the shoulders, dug her fingers in, shook me hard. She kissed me on the mouth. And then she was gone.

Morning came, with bruises on my shoulders.

She never returned for me.

It was an electrocution, a shattering.

I shut my eyes. I bit down hard. But not even that could help. I heard my own cries, felt my knees giving out.

"Not yet," she said. "Hold on. I have more to show you."

But how could I endure it?

I could die, I thought. *I could let it consume me.*

But I had so much to lose, so much I'd come to love. It broke my heart, the thought of leaving them forever. Goodbye, Lee. Goodbye to the flowers and the soft grasses. Goodbye, Julia's arm linked in mine. Goodbye to Terry's sincerity, his doubts, his warm bread, and his deep laughter. I'd taken too long, I guessed. I hadn't acted when I'd needed to, and now my chance was over. I would never be golden. I thought of Billy, teaching me to make butter, making me laugh. Liz, taking care of me, her body against mine in the tub, her press of cotton against my cut.

Somehow, my knees steadied, even as the pain coursed through me. Even as I trembled, tasted blood in my mouth, a strength I hadn't known rose up. For them, my heart still beat steadily. For them, I could withstand anything.

When you feel the hurt begin . . .

"I'm ready," I told my ghost again, and this time I was telling the truth.

One . . .

My mother, when we still lived with Grammy and
    Grandpa,
tiptoeing into our room after her shift,
kissing my forehead.

two . . .

My grandpa's cat, who licked salt off my skin
and purred and curled, warm,
to nap in the crook of my arm.

three . . .

My sixth-grade classroom.
Books and pencil shavings.
How tall I would raise my hand.

four . . .

Grammy's warm spiced milk to help me sleep.

five . . .

Afternoons in the backyard sunshine.
Shovels and soil and ferns in pots.

six . . .

The evening news. The old plaid sofa.

seven . . .

Chopping apples for pie.
Cinnamon and butter.

eight . . .

Sleepovers with Hayley, whispers after lights-out.

nine . . .

Grandpa and me, pushing the grocery cart down the
aisles.

ten

Soft sheets, my mother singing a lullaby.

I know I could
Always be good
To one
Who'll watch over me

I was lifted from the grass by many hands, placed into out-stretched arms. Someone carried me into my cabin. Some-one pulled back the sheets and tucked me in. A kiss on my forehead, a smoothing of my hair. Quiet footsteps, low murmurs.

"Think she's warm enough?"

"I'll rekindle the fire."

"Is she okay?"

"*Shhhh*. Let her sleep."

I had come to live in a haunted place. A faraway place. Once, I'd despaired at Blake slipping my phone into his pocket. But when Nick had told me there was no reception, I'd said it was okay.

I had come to live away from other people, in a place re-moved from time. In my part-sleep, part-wakefulness, alone in my silent cabin, I called back Blake's voice. I wanted to remember. *Her name was Lorna. She died last May.* And Ter-ry's, too. *I hope you aren't afraid of ghosts.*

At Blake's, I washed my hair under a spigot. At the farm, I washed my body under the sky. It's what I was told to do, so I did it.

I turned in my bed, pressed my face to the pillow.

Much later, light.

Liz stood on a chair to reach the ceiling, covered the skylight with a cloth. Julia, below, handed her pushpins. Darkness again.

A glass of water at my lips. "Just one sip and we'll let you sleep."

An ache as I swallowed.

My voice, a whisper. "Is it time for lessons?"

"No. Today is for rest."

"Today is for rest," I repeated once they were gone again.

You don't feel right, Blake had said. *Go lie down*.

Deep sleep, no dreams, pillow soft against my cheek.

Later still. No light through the curtains. Terry's hand on my shoulder.

"Can you sit up for me, Mila?"

A warm slice of bread. A mug of broth.

"Good. Good."

Blankets tucked again, door shut again, deep black sleep again.

The groan of the door, light footsteps. Weight on my bed, scent of grass. *Lee*. Quick, tight hug and then gone.

Wind through the eucalyptus leaves. Wind through the grasses.

But, no. No reason to doubt them. They had always been kind, always shown me they cared.

My high was meeting Mila.

My *high was meeting Mila.*

Thank you, I'd told them. *I'm so lucky.*

You're lucky to be here with me, Blake had said.

And the dark night, hour after hour, on and on and on.

I woke up alone. *Tap-tap* of rain on the tin roof. So cold I kept the blanket around my shoulders as I crossed to the stove. I crumpled the newsprint and lit the match. I checked the latch as I always did before leaving the cabin.

In the bathroom, I hung the blanket on the hook, stepped out of my pajamas. I stood before the mirror, expecting to see bruises on my shoulders where my mother had dug her fingers in and shaken.

But my skin was only my skin. No evidence of heartbreak.

I showered and watched the steam rise.

And then, a little later, after I had returned to my cabin, after the rain had stopped and the sun had come out, after I had dressed and combed my hair, I opened my door and saw them.

Liz and Billy. Terry and Julia. Lee. Each of them held a bouquet of flowers. They wore sadness plainly on their faces.

I gripped the doorframe.

What was this thing, swallowing me whole?

"It's grief," Terry said.

And I wept.

Liz drew me close. Billy wrapped his arms around me. Lee took my hand in his. I heard a sound, muffled at first, until Billy and Liz let me go and I realized it was Julia, speaking.

"A gift," she said, and placed a small box in my hand.

Here it was, just as I'd hoped. But I was living in a haunted place. I understood the ghosts now, but what else might I discover? So many ways, still, to be hurt. How was I to know what was right?

The box was soft velvet. It fit perfectly in my hand. But the ache in my body, the traces of blood. The ash and the tricks.

Gold earrings, stabbed into my ears.

Gold bracelets, dangling from their wrists.

"Go ahead," Liz said. "Open it."

I broke the seal and lifted the lid.

There it was.

I was in the doorway. Inside was my cabin, small and warm. Outside they were waiting in the new, bright morning.

Soon, I thought, one of them would fasten the bracelet

around my wrist. They would claim me, whether I wanted to be claimed or not.

But they stood perfectly still. No one reached for the bracelet. No one took my wrist in their hand. They waited for me, holding flowers. And I searched their faces, one and then the next.

Found I loved them almost more than I could bear.

"Mila," Julia said. "Wear this if you want to. Only if you want to. This can be your home forever, if you want it to be."

I took the chain between the tips of my fingers, lifted it to the light. Each delicate link sparkled in the sun. It would have been lovely on anyone's wrist. It would have been precious, with or without me. But it was everything I wanted, because I chose it to be mine.

Acknowledgments

Thank you to Eleanor Lonardo of The Borrowed Garden and Mel and Kyle Forrest Burns of Nye Ranch for teaching me about growing flowers and welcoming me to their farms so I could witness the beauty they've cultivated.

Stephanie Perkins, thank you for sharing your vast true crime expertise with me. Those epic text chains and podcast binges were the perfect way to begin this project.

Thank you to my writing group—Laura Joyce Davis, Teresa Miller, and Carly Ann West—for your insights and support over all these many years.

Thank you to Amanda Krampf, Brandy Colbert, Jessica Jacobs, and Nicole Kronzer for your invaluable feedback on my drafts, and for your friendship, too.

This novel wouldn't be what it is without Elana K. Arnold, who talked me through so many struggles and off so many ledges, and gave me the ideas for some of its best moments.

Thank you to Sara Crowe, my generous and steadfast agent and friend. I'm ever fortunate to have you in my corner. And thank you to all of Pippin Properties—what an incredible team you are.

Julie Strauss-Gabel, you pushed me hard on this one. I won't say it was easy, but I wouldn't have it any other way. Thank you for helping this book (and all the others) become the best versions of themselves, and for the care you put into every step of the process. Thank you, also, to my entire Penguin family, who I appreciate more than I can say. From making my novels look so beautiful inside and out to ensuring they reach as many readers as they can, I am so grateful.

This novel is coming out in the midst of a global pandemic—something many of us never imagined we'd live through. Thank you to my wife Kristyn, my anchor and my love. Thank you to my daughter Juliet for keeping me playing and laughing and snuggling and marveling.

As I'm writing these acknowledgments, it's been months since I've seen the rest of my family and friends in person. I miss you terribly. I hope you know how much I love you. Thank you—my family of origin, my family through marriage, and my family of friends—for being mine to choose.